D0399263

JENNIFER MASCHARI

THINGS THAT SURPRISE YOU

BALZER + BRAY
An Imprint of HarperCollins*Publishers*

HarperCollins
PUBLISHERS

Balzer + Bray is an imprint of HarperCollins Publishers.

Things That Surprise You
Text copyright © 2017 by Jennifer Maschari
All rights reserved. Printed in the United States of America. No part of
this book may be used or reproduced in any manner whatsoever without
written permission except in the case of brief quotations embodied in
critical articles and reviews. For information address HarperCollins
Children's Books, a division of HarperCollins Publishers, 195 Broadway,
New York, NY 10007.
www.harpercollinschildrens.com

ISBN 978-0-06-243892-8

Typography by Andrea Vandergrift
17 18 19 20 21   CG/LSCH   10 9 8 7 6 5 4 3 2 1
❖
First Edition

For Lauren

SUMMER US

Glitter is everywhere.

It's sticking to the tops of my summer-burned toes, which still have flecks of blue polish from the last time Hazel painted them. It's on the faded green and pink rug in my room where I'm sitting cross-legged. There's a little bit of glitter on the top of Bean's brown head, too, right next to her bald spot. I'm trying to decorate the construction paper unicorn horn that I've stapled together. Things are always messier than I expect.

There are two knocks at the front door. A pause. Then the doorbell rings. Even if I wasn't expecting Hazel, I'd know it was her just from that. "Mom!" I yell. She's actually home today instead of at the bank. "Can you get it?"

Mom's footsteps echo down the hall and then pound against the wooden stairs. The door opens. Bean jumps up to follow behind, even though she knows who it's going to be, too. Everything about Hazel is loud and clattery—like a cymbal clashing. Her voice carries. I hear Mom ask if she wants something to drink (no) and if she's excited about school starting (new school: yes, homework: no). By the time Mom's yelled, "Emily, it's Hazel," she's already up in my room and face-planting onto my bed like she's doing a belly flop into the deep end of the neighborhood pool.

I think she says hello, but it's pretty muffled because she's speaking into my comforter.

The bed creaks as she rolls over. "Ugh," she groans.

"Ugh?" I'm still concentrating.

"We did sprints today. My legs are noodles."

"Hmm."

"There's still time for you to join," she says hopefully. "Games don't start till school does."

"Gym class last year," I remind her.

She sighs, probably remembering how I came last in the mile run. "Right."

I'm still decorating the horn. I sprinkle the last bit of glitter onto the glue swirl and wave it around in the air a little so it dries faster. It's perfect, like I've captured little bits of the sun. It looks exactly like Nightshade's horn on the cover of the latest Unicorn Chronicles book. The one that's coming out today. I glance at my watch. In exactly one hour.

When I finally look up at Hazel, though, I'm not thinking about her noodle legs or the horn in my hand. "Your hair!" The words just slip out. I hope I've said it in a nice-surprise way and not a bad-surprise way. Her usual light brown hair has thin streaks of blond in it like someone's painted them on with a brush. Hazel sits up on the bed and pulls out her ponytail holder, shaking her hair out. Her hair's shorter now, too, cut straight at her shoulders.

"Do you like it?" Hazel asks. She pulls a strand through her fingertips.

"It's so fancy," I say. And it is—even though she's just been running at field hockey tryouts, her hair still looks bouncy and shiny, like the picture she showed me in *Teen Scene*. It doesn't look anything like a summer ago when we spritzed on lemon juice, and Hazel's hair turned a strange shade of orange till it grew all the way out.

"Mom took me to the salon yesterday. Andi says she's given three haircuts just like mine this week. And when we were leaving, one of the ladies up front told me I looked totally different." She grins. "I think I do, too."

I don't know why but my face starts to feel a little flushy.

"I think you kind of look the same."

Her grin fades.

"No, you know what I mean," I rush in. "You always look great."

That puts the spring back into her. "So when are we leaving?" she asks. "I gotta find out what happens."

"As soon as you're ready! Where's your costume?" I look around. Maybe she left her bag downstairs or is planning to change once we get to the bookstore.

"I'm sorry, Em." She doesn't look directly at me. "I didn't have time to make anything. You know. Practice and stuff."

My heart skips a little. I'm thinking that maybe all the time that went into texting me pictures of a possible first-day-of-school outfit could have been used to make a costume instead. But I don't say that. Last year, we spent a week on the floor of Hazel's room sewing sweatshirts together and made a giant eyeball out of papier-mâché to be the Cyclops of Doom. Last year, we won first place in the costume contest and got our picture on the front page of the newspaper.

This year Hazel has on her running shorts with the funky stripe down the side and her official Eleanor Roosevelt Middle School Field Hockey practice shirt and her sneakers. All that would normally be fine, except none of the characters in the Unicorn Chronicles books wear any of those things.

I get an idea. "I think Mina has a T-shirt from last year you could wear!"

I jump up and race out of the room and into Mina's across the hall before Hazel can say anything. There are fresh lines on the carpet from where Mom's vacuumed. I feel bad for getting my footprints all over, but Mom will just vacuum again tomorrow. She'll dust off the stuff Mina's collected on her bookshelves: shells from the beach and jazz choir awards and her collection of weird key chains. All things that make it look like a real live person is living there but isn't. Mom wants Mina's room to be clean and ready and perfect for when she comes home.

I root around in Mina's bottom drawer where she keeps her old shirts. Right underneath the one that says *Ithaca Is Gorges*, I find the one I'm looking for and hold it out in front of me. It has a picture of Nightshade with her detective hat. She's holding up a magnifying glass with her hoof. The magnifying part is still shiny. The back says *The Unicorn Chronicles Magical Mystery Tour*.

It should fit Hazel. Hazel and Mina used to be about the same size.

"I've got it!" I call. "And I bet I have an extra horn from last year you could wear. Remember? From our Halloween costumes?"

"I think just the shirt—" she says, but now I'm already back in my room and going through a bin at the bottom of my closet. I find one. It's a little bit crumpled but it's purple, like the horn of Nightshade's best friend, Starlight.

I hand both of them to her.

There's a moment where she's holding the things in her hand and just looking at them. The tiniest bit of worry settles under my skin. But she turns toward the wall and slips out of the one shirt and into the other and I exhale. Then she pulls the elastic band attached to the horn tight and slips it under her chin. Just like before with the hair, she changes again, but this time to something more familiar. I swish my detective cape around my shoulders and tie it at my neck. I stuff the rest of my frizzy hair into Nightshade's detective cap. I've sliced open the top of it so the unicorn horn can stick out.

We crowd into the view of the small mirror over my dresser. Hazel squeezes my hand. It's summer us. Freckle-dotted. Matching lime green Popsicle earrings in our June-pierced ears. My orange soda–stained smile and Hazel's that's coated in the Very Berry lip gloss she got at the mall last week.

In five days, it's going to be middle school us.

As a last-minute thought, I sprinkle a little bit of the remaining glitter onto the top of each of our heads.

Hazel winces, maybe because of her perfect new hair. But then she must see what I see, how the bits of glitter are like little pieces of light.

She grins now. "Perfect!"

✳ ✳ ✳

By the time Mom's taken our picture together on the front step and we've ridden the back way to the bookstore and tied up our bikes to the rack, the line for the Unicorn Chronicles book party is stretched halfway around the building. Also, there are two puddles of sweat that have formed underneath my armpits because I'm riding around in white sweatpants and a sweatshirt when it's August hot in Ohio.

Hazel sighs a little bit when she looks at the line. "I wish Mina were here." Last year, Mina drove us to the bookstore with her new license. She had rolled the windows down and me and Hazel made up car dance moves to the songs that blared from the speakers. Last year, we arrived so early that we were at the very front of the line.

"Yeah," I say, but I don't want to talk about Mina right now. I want to talk about unicorns and Nightshade and eating pizza afterward. I feel like a little bit of the glitter's been shaken off the day. "The line will move fast! It won't take long at all."

Hazel bounces on the toes of her sneakers, her focus shifted. We've waited a little over a year for this. A year spent on the Unicorn Underworld fan forum and combing through books one through five trying to find any kind of clue that would reveal Nightshade's fate.

In line, we're stuck between a dad with a kid on his back who keeps making faces at us and an older lady who seems very confused about why there's a line and a bunch of people dressed up like mythical creatures. "Okay, new theory," Hazel says, thinking aloud. "What if Disastero is really Nightshade's father?"

"No way!" I say. "Why would Disastero try to kill her then?"

Hazel shrugs. "He doesn't know." She spins around excitedly. "Or *maybe* he does but knows that Nightshade is close to revealing the secrets of the Hidden Kingdom? What about that?"

I turn her words over in my mind. At the end of the last book, Nightshade and Disastero were fighting on the edge of a cliff with Nightshade dangling over the side, holding on by only one hoof. "It could be. There were lots of chances for him to get rid of her before. Maybe there's a reason he hasn't."

"Exactly!"

"You're brilliant, Starlight."

Hazel winks at me. "You're spectacular, Nightshade."

The minutes start to add up. We're waiting in line longer than I had anticipated. The sun seems even hotter than before. I can feel my hair getting soggy and gross under my cap, and the elastic of the horn is cutting into my chin. I rub my hand underneath it but I don't want to take it off. Hazel's getting impatient, I can tell, even though they're pumping music from the Nightshade movie soundtrack over the speakers. Her answers to my book questions are shorter now—a yes or a no or a maybe. But I know it's only because it's hot and the line is long and she's hungry for our favorite pizza at the Slice. Once we get inside the bookstore and into the air-conditioning with the books in our hands, everything will be fine.

"Okay, three middle school things you're excited about." It's a game we play—just the two of us. You pick a category and then name three things: vacations you want to take or your most favorite foods or your favorite jokes.

Hazel brightens and I feel my shoulders relax.

"Eeee!" she says. "Good one. Just three things? Okay—lockers. One hundred percent lockers. Playing field hockey. And . . ." Her eyes roll up like she's thinking really hard. "It's totally new."

"Totally new?" Of all the things she could have picked—the cafeteria breadstick bar or the big class field trip to the ball game in the spring or anything really—she picked that?

"Yeah—think about it. No one knows us. Well, some people but not many. We could totally be someone different. Like you could be Em."

"Em?" I'm echoing back things Hazel's saying right now because it's like I've learned something new and different and strange about her. I like Hazel the way she is and can't imagine this brand new Middle School Hazel.

"Yeah!" She grabs my arm and leans in like she's sharing a secret. "Em Murphy. It sounds so cool, doesn't it? Em Murphy, who wears Very Berry lip gloss and knows the best dance moves and writes her name in fancy-pants cursive." She pretends to write my name in the air with extra squiggles. "How does that sound?"

"Cool?" I hate the way my voice goes up. I try again. "Cool." I think it could be very cool.

"Middle school is going to be so different. But so great, you know?" The line starts moving then and Hazel goes back to talking about Nightshade, so I don't get to say my three things, which is good because I can think of only one: spending sixth grade together with Hazel.

SHIFTS

The inside of the bookstore is loud. It's packed full of bumpy elbows and "excuse me's" and older kids. Even kids I recognize from Mina's grade. Brightly colored balloons bounce against the ceiling. There are trays with unicorn sugar cookies and a bowl of bright green leprechaun punch that I always have too many cups of.

A giant cardboard cutout of Nightshade in her detective clothes is set up in front of a white sheet. One of the bookstore staff members stands in front of it with a Polaroid camera.

Walking in here is like stepping into a pair of the fuzziest socks. It feels cozy and right.

"There it is!" Hazel says, pointing to stacks and stacks of books piled up on a table in the front of the store. I grin. My stomach feels like it's fizzy with Pop Rocks.

They have two mini spotlights trained on a table in the front that flash alternating blues and yellows. Hazel and I weave through the crowd. She hands me a book off the stack and then grabs another one for herself.

"Don't even think about reading the end," Hazel says, smiling. She somehow knows, even though she's reading the inside flap and isn't even looking at me. I stop mid-flip, my cheeks flushing.

"You caught me." I laugh it off and close the book. It's a bad habit I have.

Because I'm not reading the end, I'm looking around. There's a kid—way shorter than me—who has his back against one of the shelves. He has these thick glasses and black hair that's sticking up like the quills of a porcupine. Green paint covers his arms and face. His shirt is ripped at the bottom like his body is too big for it, and he has on matching green and purple high tops.

"The ogre," I whisper. It's maybe the best ogre costume I've seen. And believe it or not, I've seen a lot of them. Half the kids I saw out last year for Halloween were Unicorn Chronicles characters.

"What?" Hazel asks. She's already flipped to the front page.

"He's the ogre," I say. "From book two."

The ogre kid hears me, because he looks up from his book and grins. "Nice costume," he says.

There's a girl next to him—same green paint and same black hair, but hers is longer and split into two matching braids. "Your horn looks great." She holds up the book, marking her place in it with her finger. "Almost an exact match." She nods approvingly.

"Is it Disastero?" I ask. "Is he really the Unicorn King?" I can see that they're both already twenty pages in and certainly they've found out what happened to Nightshade on the cliff by now.

I feel a hand on my back. "Emily," Hazel says in a low voice. "I'm ready to go."

"What? Wait. We just got here."

Hazel raises her eyebrows at me and I think she's trying to communicate without words, but I'm not really sure of the message. There's air-conditioning in here and unicorn cookies and I haven't even had any punch yet.

"Hold up," I say. "I mean, he's got to be, right?" I strain forward to peek at the page.

The boy opens his mouth to speak.

"No, stop," I say. "Don't tell me anything. Okay, maybe something. Wink once if he is, twice if he's not."

Hazel has grabbed my hand now, but I plant my feet. The ogre blinks.

"You blinked. Does that count as two winks or is it supposed to be a single wink?"

"Em," Hazel says. I can tell she's getting impatient. "You'll get to read it tonight."

"Is that your name?" the girl says. She looks like the boy. They have the same crooked smile. I bet she's his sister. "Em? Like the letter?"

I could correct her and say that my name is Emily, but maybe new names need to be broken in, like a pair of jeans. Emily was my fifth-grade name. I wonder if I've outgrown it.

"It's *really* good so far," the boy says as Hazel pulls me away. "And Disastero *is* in the first chapter. . . ." His voice trails off.

Hazel ducks her head toward mine as we walk away. She's so close that our unicorn horns touch. "That was Soap Boy."

"Who?" I'm not sure why only questions are coming out of my mouth today. "Soap Boy? What kind of name is that?"

"A name you don't want! His actual name is Hector, but no one calls him that. Lucy said they put a bar of soap in his desk on the last day of elementary."

"Lucy? Field hockey team Lucy?"

Hazel nods.

"Why would she do that?"

At this Hazel bristles. "I don't know. I guess he smelled

bad. I wasn't there. Anyway, it was just a joke, you know. It wasn't serious or anything." She turns away from me.

"I'm sure," I say lightly. I touch her sleeve. "A joke."

The moment of tension disappears. Hazel's relaxed and smiley again.

Phoebe Chen is behind the counter at the register—Mina's Work Best Friend. She has a neon-green stripe in her hair and a little jewel on the side of her nose. They're new things but not surprising. Phoebe just seems even more Phoebe than before. "Hey, girl!" she exclaims. She reaches across the counter and squeezes my hand. "I'd come around and give you a hug but we're a little busy." She gestures at the line that's formed behind us, almost everyone holding their very own copy of book six: *Nightshade and the Mystery of the Moaning Moat*. She's wearing her red and white *The Book Nook* shirt. Hers has streaks of permanent marker and dried bits of icing from the cookies. Mina has one, too, but hers is folded up, clean and laundered in her T-shirt drawer, right next to the Ithaca one.

She scans my book. "Seventeen twenty-five." I pull out a wad of money from my pocket and count out eighteen dollars. "Have you talked to Mina lately? Do you think she's coming home soon?"

Hazel looks up from the teen magazine she's been flipping through. "What?" she asks. "Is she? You didn't tell me."

"No," I say. "I don't know. I mean, it could be soon." My stomach twists up tight.

"Oh," Hazel says. She goes back to reading.

Back in July, it was supposed to be two weeks. Then two days. But Dr. Oliver, Mina's therapist from Pinehurst, talked to Mom and said she wasn't quite ready to come home yet. So Mina stayed. Her Book Nook T-shirt stayed in the drawer and her room stayed clean and unlived in. I took down the remaining links in the countdown chain I had hung along my ceiling and threw them away.

"It has to be soon," I say, eager to end the conversation. Somehow, talking about it feels like I'll jinx it. I take my bag and my change from Phoebe.

Then I wait for Hazel, who buys the magazine, too.

It's still early, so the Slice isn't crowded at all—a few old people and a family eating at the big table near the window. I slide into our favorite booth in the back. The table's a little lopsided and a big chunk of fabric's missing from the seat, but it's the closest one to the jukebox. It's one of the old-fashioned kinds that still play records.

"What do you want to hear?" Hazel's pressing the buttons to flip through the selections, her hips swaying to some imaginary beat. "Ooh, wait—got it."

The drums start and Hazel grabs a straw off the table

and holds it to her face like a microphone. "Hang on Sloopy, Sloopy hang on." She mouths the words along with the song and when we get to the part right after the chorus, we raise our hands in the air: "O-H-I-O." She laughs and falls into the other side of the booth.

A teen boy appears at the table wearing an *A Slice of Heaven* ball cap. He flips open a notepad. "What'll it be?"

I'm about to say the regular—Kitchen Sink pizza, extra cheese, and a pitcher of orange soda to split—when Hazel picks up the menu that's tucked behind the napkin dispenser. "I think we need a minute." She grins at him with her lip-glossed lips.

The boy steps away. She kicks my sneaker under the table and kind of gestures in his direction with a nod. "He's cute."

"Yeah," I say. "And seventeen or something. He practically has a mustache." He looks older than Mina. "Aren't we getting what we always get?"

"I don't know." Her words are long and slow. "Don't you think it might be fun to get something new? We always get the Kitchen Sink. Let's try something different."

"But it's our favorite."

Hazel shrugs. "I mean, it's good, but shouldn't we try something a little healthier? Like veggie?" She turns her menu and points at the picture, as if somehow that will convince me. "Doesn't that look good?"

What it looks like is a portable salad, but I don't say that.

I open a menu of my own and hold it out to her. "The Kitchen Sink pizza. Yum." I move the menu in a circle like I'm hypnotizing her. "You are getting very hungry. Very, very hungry."

Hazel's not having it. "Okay, why don't we do this? I'll get the veggie and you get whatever you want and we'll split it." Hazel and I split food all the time—half of my peanut butter and jelly for half of her turkey with avocado, half of my chips for half of her Oreos (cream side). So even though we're not eating the Kitchen Sink together, that sounds okay to me.

The boy comes back. "Ready now?" he asks.

"I'll have a water. And a personal veggie pizza," Hazel says. "No onions."

"Um, small sausage and onion." The words feel weird coming out of my mouth. "With an orange soda."

While Hazel and I wait, we bench dance to the music from the jukebox. It's a lot like car dancing but a little more restrained since you're in public and everything. She does the squid, a move she made up where you wiggle your arms on either side of your body. I do the turtle, where you bob your head forward and backward. Hazel's snort-laughing and I practically have tears coming out of my eyes, when I hear a noise behind me. Hazel stops dancing. I turn my head to look, but not so fast that I miss Hazel taking the purple horn off her head and hiding it below the table. I blink once and then again. Confused.

"Hazel!" the voice cries but it really sounds like "Heyyyyyzel" the way she draws it out.

Three girls wearing the same field hockey shirt Hazel was before crowd around the booth.

"What are you doing here?" the tallest one asks. I think the answer is pretty obvious; we are at a pizza place after all.

"We were just out and stopped to get something to eat," Hazel says. "Come sit with us. That's okay, right?" But she doesn't wait for my answer. I grab my bag and bike helmet to make room. Two of the girls squish in next to me so that I'm now sitting on the missing chunk. I sink down lower. The tall girl sits next to Hazel. I bet that's Lucy.

"Everyone, this is Em." I smile a little and can't seem to stop blinking. "This is Lucy and Annemarie and Gina." They all look totally different—Lucy with her straight black hair and Annemarie with her tiny eyebrows, and Gina with her jangly bracelets stacked up on her left arm. But at the same time, they all kind of look alike, too. Maybe it's the funky shorts or the knee-high socks or their hair up in ponytails. They look like a team even off the field.

Lucy turns to me. She looks me up and down. A small smile forms on her face. "A little early for Halloween."

My cheeks flush. "Well—" I start. "It's—" But the right words aren't forming.

"It was this thing at the bookstore," Hazel rushes in. "For the Unicorn Chronicles."

"Oh, that's cool," Lucy says. "What are you supposed to be?"

I grin and try to sit up straighter. "I'm Nightshade. The main unicorn detective."

Lucy turns her attention to Hazel. "Isn't Drew Lewis supposed to be in the next movie? When does that come out?"

I try to meet eyes with Hazel, but she's not looking at me. "November, I think."

I jump in. "Drew Lewis *is* in it. He's the magician's apprentice. And it comes out September 30th." It's on my calendar. Hazel has it circled on hers, too. "Me and Hazel are going together."

"Oh yeah," Hazel says.

The teen boy returns, but this time with our pizzas and drinks. "Orange soda and sausage and onion." He sets down the food in front of me. "And a water and veggie."

"Do you guys want any?" I ask. I hold the little paper plates like an offering.

Annemarie shakes her head. "No, thanks. We'll eat later, right?" She looks at Lucy and smiles when she nods in agreement.

Hazel blots her pizza with a napkin and holds it up. It's shiny with grease. She's removing the best part. The air feels hotter now somehow, even though there's a fan right above us.

"That's very unhealthy," Lucy says. She wrinkles her nose and Hazel nods in agreement. "Hey, dare me to hit the server with this straw paper."

Annemarie laughs. "Do it."

But I'm not watching the stuff with the straws; instead I'm concentrating on how Hazel's delicately spearing one of her super-small pieces with her fork. My heart thumps in my chest. Before Mina left, she used to cut her food up into tiny pieces and then move them around the plate but not really eat anything at all. At least some of Hazel's pieces are disappearing. I take a deep breath.

I go to take a bite of my own pizza, crust first, when Gina's elbow hits my hand. The pizza slides down on the sleeve of my sweatshirt, leaving a trail of sausage bits and cheese strings.

"Sorry," she says. "But look at that aim." The straw paper she's just shot has landed on top of the jukebox. I watch it flutter in place. She holds her hand out to me. "High five." I hit her hand with mine. She holds a straw out. "Want to see if you can shoot it even farther?"

I just took a giant pizza bite, so I shake my head no. I'm feeling good. Hazel's been talking about these girls all August and it'll be good that we know some new people going in. Of course, it'll still be Hazel and me, but we can't just sit alone together at a lunch table. If Hazel asked me again, I'd add these new friends to the list of things I'm excited about.

After talking about field hockey practice and first-quarter schedules and some kid named Joey's skateboarding skills, the girls leave and Hazel bounces up-down in her seat.

"I knew you'd love them," she says. "And Gina always comes to practice with these awesome braids. Maybe she'll teach us. I think my hair's still long enough."

"That would be great," I say. I try to imagine where three more girls will fit into Hazel's tiny room for sleepovers.

"I knew they'd like you, *Em Murphy*." She exaggerates my name like I'm some kind of queen or celebrity. "Hey! Do you have two quarters? I wanna play one more song." I pull two quarters out of my pocket and hand them to her. The server's already boxed up our pizzas to go. We never did get to trade.

"I'm going to go to the bathroom," I say.

Even through the bathroom door, though, I can hear the refrain of the song Hazel chose. We spent hours up in her bedroom watching the YouTube video for it on repeat so we could get the dance moves just right.

I wonder if Annemarie and Gina and Lucy like to dance, too. I picture all of us dancing in sync.

By the time I step out, Hazel's waiting for me outside the restaurant.

I pluck the straw wrapper off the jukebox and another one off the floor and throw them into the trash can. Then I grab my leftovers, bag, and bike helmet and walk out the door.

NEW TEEN TRENDS

I decide I need a back-to-school outfit, too.

Mom's still in her bank clothes since she's picked me up straight from work. White blouse, too-tan panty hose, and maroon skirt, which she says makes a good impression. I think it must, because the bank has given her more hours.

She does change into gym shoes when we get to the mall, though. She keeps them in the backseat because she has to stand in these pinch-toed heels all day, and she says she's still not used to it.

I hold the door open for her. The chill of the air-conditioning feels good against my skin. There's nothing awesome about August weather.

"So what are you thinking?" Mom asks. We're heading to the juniors section on the second floor. There's a bunch of people here. Maybe they all want back-to-school outfits, just like me. Hazel says that clothes say something about you without you having to even open your mouth. I think she read it in *Teen Scene*, but she's right. If sixth grade is going to be a brand new start, then I need something that says EM!

"I'm not really sure. Something cute and fun," I say, trying out the words Hazel texted me about her own outfits.

"Hmm, cute and fun." Mom heads straight for the sales rack while I hang back and look at the display with *New Teen Trends* written over the top of it in neon glowing letters. I pick up a shirt and hold it out in front of me.

"What do you think?" I ask.

Mom shakes her head. "I don't know, Emily. It's a little mature." Maybe it is, but that's kind of what I want. It's cropped at the waist, so I'm thinking my belly button would probably show. I picture it—a stripe of pale, freckly skin right over my jeans. My hand reaches for my stomach to cover it as if it were a reflex. Hazel would tell me to get it. I put it back.

Mom flips through a bunch of shirts. She pulls one out. "Why don't you try this one on?" From the back, it looks like a plain old T-shirt, but the front is covered in gold sparkly polka dots. "Maybe with your magenta pants? And a little navy blue sweater? Those school buildings are cold."

I close my eyes and think. Is it something that brand new sixth-grade Em Murphy would wear? I'm not sure.

The saleslady lets me into the dressing room. I slide the shirt on and open the door. I'm quick, so Mom's not paying attention yet. She's sitting on one of the faded fabric chairs that has week-old cherry slushy stains or something on it. Her head is back against the wall and her eyes are closed and she's doing this thing where she kneads her eyebrows together with her hand. She looks the most tired I've ever seen her. My face grows warm. This moment feels like the one when I saw Mina kissing Hugo Morris on the back deck two summers ago—a hidden one. Private and secret and something I'm not supposed to see. I close the door as quietly as I can and try to forget it happened.

I count to three in my head. "Okay, Mom. I'm coming out," I announce this time. Loud.

Now Mom's leaning forward. She's smiling big like that last moment of tiredness never happened. "Emily, that looks darling on you."

I have to say, it's not bad. But I'm not sure if it's not bad in a Mom-picked-it-out kind of way, or if it's not bad in an it's-actually-cute-and-fun kind of way. But there's just me and Mom here and no one else to ask.

"You're looking so grown-up these days." She says it in a way that's happy and sad at the same time.

You can't go to the mall without getting the good soft pretzels from the food court. I get mine with dipping cheese and Mom gets hers with extra salt.

Mom brushes crumbs off a table with a napkin, and we sit down. We're quiet for a minute, just eating and chewing and listening to two lovebird teens five tables down from us talk loudly about how adorable the other one is. Mom's phone buzzes. All other noises—the little kids screeching at the play place, the elevator music piped in above, the crumpling of paper food wrappers—fade into the background. "It's Dr. Oliver." She takes in a sharp breath and clicks the button to take the call. "I'll be right back."

Mom walks away from the table. I put my pretzel down.

Even though Mina's not *here*, she's here. She's everywhere. It's like her Converse sneakers are propped up on the chair next to me here in the food court. For once, I wanted it to be me and Mom. I only want to think about my back-to-school shirt that's in the bag between my sneakers and the silver unicorn earrings Mom added to the pile at the register at the last minute. I only want to think about Em Murphy, world's best sixth grader. I want to think about locker decorations and me and Hazel together in the cafeteria. I want

27

to be 100 percent happy about something—not 88 or 74 or whatever percentage I am right now.

Selfish, my brain says. *You're so selfish*. My stomach twists with guilt.

Mom's back now. "Guess what?" She doesn't wait for me to answer. "Mina's coming home!" She's grinning, but I can't meet her eyes.

I should smile. Or give Mom a hug. Instead I say, "That's what you said last time." It's the wrong thing to say but the only thing I can think of. I picture the Welcome Home decorations I had made back in July, now shoved away in the bottom of my art bin.

Mom can't seem to keep still. "I think it's really going to happen." She takes a big sip of her giant Diet Coke in celebration. "Things have gone really well this past week. She thinks Mina's ready. Mina thinks she's ready."

I hold in a big sigh. A little bit of me *is* excited. But the excitement is so mixed up with nervousness and grumpiness that it gets a little lost. "That's so great," I say, but the words sound fake.

Mom looks down now and sees my almost uneaten pretzel. "Oh, honey," she says. "Are you worried about school starting? It's going to be okay. You love school."

I nod but don't look up. I don't want Mom to see my feelings about Mina all over my face.

* * *

Later that evening, I'm sitting on the back porch with a glass of lemonade. Well, what used to be lemonade. Now it's only melty lemon water and I'm drawing pictures in the condensation with my finger.

Dad promised he'd call at eight. My cell phone finally rings a half hour later.

"Hey, Dad," I say. The screen door to the house is open, and every so often Mom walks past. She's got her soft slippers on but I can still hear her. Our house is a nice quiet right now.

"Hold on a second there," Dad says. In the background, there's the whirr of the can opener and the clink of a metal bowl. "Sorry about that. I had to feed Pickle." Pickle is Alice's cat. And now Dad's cat, too, I guess. I never knew Dad was a cat person. "So what's up, kiddo? Tell me what's going on with you."

"Hazel and I went to this bookstore thing," I say. "Mom got me new—"

"Speaking of new," Dad interrupts. "Alice and I got a new couch. . . ." I tune out when he mentions her. *Blah, blah, blah* Alice. *Blah, blah, blah.* Then he asks me a question. "You still like purple, right?"

"Purple?" I try to make it sound like I've been paying attention.

"Yeah, the color Alice wants to paint your new room."

I frown. "But I already have a room. It's already painted."

"I know that, Button. But Alice thought that this might—" Every time he says her name my chest squeezes a little tighter.

"I don't actually like purple anymore, Dad."

"Oh, really?" Dad sounds less excited now. I feel a little bad. "Well, that's okay. When you come next weekend, we can pick out paint together. Any color you want. We'll have a painting party. Me, you, and Alice. Won't that be great?"

"Sure." There's silence. "Mina's coming home in a week."

Dad's quiet. I hear Alice in the background, the hum of the fan over the stove, the clinking of pans. They must be cooking together. "Your mother told me," he says after a minute. "That's great. It seems like Mina's really doing well." I wonder if he's nervous like I am.

"Are you coming to Mina's family thing tomorrow?" I ask.

There's another long pause. Finally, he lets out a big sigh. "I don't think I can. You know I would if I could, right?" I don't answer. I also don't feel quite as bad for being mean to him before.

"Hey, Alice wants to say hello. Do you have—"

I can't even believe him. "I gotta go, Dad."

"I'll give Mina a call this week. You tell her that, okay?"

My heart contracts. "Sure."

"Love you," he says. I click the end call button extra hard. I walk out into the yard and join Bean, who's snoozing on the last little patch of sunshine. I lay my cheek against hers. It doesn't make me feel all the way better, though.

PINEHURST

"Cookout at my house!" Hazel texts me the night before the first day of school. "Come over?"

"Can't," I reply with a frown face emoji. I don't explain further or bother asking Mom. I know what the answer will be. Wednesday evenings are for visiting Mina.

Mina's at a place called Pinehurst. It looks like it could be a summer camp if you just glance at it from the main road. There's a low-to-the-ground wooden sign that has the name written in dark green cursive letters. A gravel path winds through tall pine trees to the main campus where Mina and nineteen other girls stay.

It's not really a camp at all.

Driving there takes the same amount of time as it does to get to the Magic Castle mini-golf course and the hiking trails near the river. But Mina might as well be in Florida or Oregon for as far away as she feels. It isn't like having Mina home, in the bedroom just across the hall.

"We're lucky there's a place like Pinehurst so close," I heard Mom say into the phone one night. She was on the front porch talking to Aunt Bea, where I'm sure she thought I couldn't hear her.

She uses the word *lucky* a lot.

Lucky that Dad has pretty good insurance.

Lucky that her extra bank hours make up for the rest.

I'm feeling anything but lucky as I sit in this small room off the main hallway. It smells weird and sterile, like a hospital, even though it technically isn't. I thought I would've gotten used to it by now.

I'm sitting on a sofa. It's a faded yellow and the fabric scratches at my legs right where my shorts end. Across from me is Dr. Oliver, who told me I could call her Evie the first time we all met together seven weeks ago. She's a psychologist but she doesn't look like one. She's wearing jeans and a flannel shirt and sneakers that I'm pretty sure Hazel would love.

Mom and Mina are in the cafeteria for dinner. It's like a school cafeteria—trays and not-so-great food—but it's also different because in a school cafeteria, there aren't people watching you eat to make sure you finish everything.

Evie's across from me on a spinny office chair. Her hands are folded in her lap.

"We could walk down there together," she says. She says this every time. "I think Mina would love to have you join her."

I bite down on my left thumbnail and look out the window.

I think about the last time we went out to dinner before Mina went away. We were at China Bistro, which is in the same strip mall as Mom's bank. It smelled delicious, and I really should've been hungry, but all I felt was nauseous. I used to love Chinese food. Our favorite was Happy Family. Mina would call that ironic.

Mom asked what we wanted and Mina didn't say anything. I only shrugged. So Mom ordered our usual.

When the food came out, Mom dished some of the meat and veggies onto Mina's plate and pushed it toward her. Mina stared at it and then pushed the plate away with the tip of her finger. "I'm not hungry," she said. I couldn't understand how Mina wasn't hungry all the time.

Mom's eyes got red and watery. Suddenly, my chest felt tight. I stabbed a piece of chicken with my fork. "This is amazing," I said, taking a bite. "Wow, it's really, really good."

I pretended like I hadn't eaten an afternoon snack and kept shoveling bite after bite into my mouth until I was way past full and my shorts were starting to feel snug at my stomach.

Mina stood up. "I'll wait outside." She didn't wait for permission.

Mom turned and gave me a look like this was all somehow my fault, even though I was just trying to make things better. I set my fork down. "Mina, please," she called, but Mina didn't even turn around. I watched as she pushed the front door open hard, the bell jangling angrily.

Mom didn't even ask the waiter to box up the rest.

I look away from the window and shake my head. I'm glad I'm not in the cafeteria with Mom and Mina.

Evie leans back. "Tell me, Emily," she says. She pauses. "What do you think things will be like when Mina comes home?"

I stop biting on my nail because it's red and raw now and there is no nail left. I slip my hand beneath my thigh.

"Better." I say it because I don't understand how things could get any worse.

"What does better mean to you?"

I shrug. It's almost become automatic. But unlike when Mom's in here and she rushes in to fill the quiet, Evie just waits. "Mina will be normal," I say after a moment. "She'll eat again." I don't add: *without crying.* I don't say: *without*

*yelling so loud that Bean will no longer sit under the kitchen
table at dinnertime.*

Evie nods like that was exactly what she expected me to
say. "Mina's made great progress here. But it's important that
we all understand something."

What she means is that it's important I understand
something.

"It's not like Mina has strep throat or the chicken
pox that a little bit of time and some medicine can cure.
Pinehurst is wonderful, but it's a *start*. There's still a lot of
work that Mina's going to have to do. It's a process."

We look at each other for a moment. Maybe she's waiting for me to nod or smile or something. When I don't, she
says, "I want you to think of it this way. Mina's trying to
scale a mountain right now. We've just given her some of the
tools to help her do it."

I don't understand why she has to take us along with her.
My heart flutters with panic for a second, like Evie can see
into my brain where this terrible thought has taken shape.
But her face hasn't changed.

When Mina and Mom come in, Mina sits on the other end
of the couch. She curls her legs underneath her and leans
against the armrest. It's the absolute farthest she can be away
while still sitting next to me. Today, she hides in a sweatshirt

that hangs on her like a tent. *College of Wooster*, it says in white block letters. She got it at a college visit last spring with Mom. The visits had to stop when she got even worse.

On good days she'll look at me and say hello and she'll smile like she used to.

Today her hair hangs like a curtain around her face. She looks down.

Mina. Not Mina.

Evie reads Mina's mood and Mom's, whose eyes are red-rimmed and tired. My hands start to sweat.

"Mina, I'm getting some signals from you that things are not okay right now." Evie uses the same soft, quiet voice she used on me. "Do you want to talk to us about it? We're here to listen."

Mina looks up and around. She rolls her eyes. "Where's Dad?" Mom and Evie exchange a look.

"Your dad had to work tonight," Mom says. "He couldn't get off." Couldn't. Wouldn't. I decide that now is not the best time to pass along Dad's message. "He's sorry about it."

"I bet," she mutters.

"Is that what's bothering you?" Evie asks.

Mina's hands curl into tight fists. "What's bothering me is that you're trying to make me fat." Her voice shakes. "I feel gross today."

I should reach my hand out to her, but instead I start

picking at a loose thread on one of the couch cushions.

It starts to unravel. It's strangely satisfying watching the thread unspool. I pull harder.

"I'm hearing you say that today was hard," Evie says. She makes a note on her clipboard.

Mina bounces up on her legs now, like she can barely stand her skin. She's perched on the cushion like a bird. "Every day is hard." Her words echo off the walls. She turns her sharp gaze to me. My hand freezes. "God, Emily. Stop that. It's annoying." I look down at my lap.

"Do you think she's really ready to come home?" Mom asks Evie. I can hear the worry in her voice.

"Mom!" Mina exclaims. "I'm right here. Say it to me. Ask me."

Mom rubs her hands against her pants. "Mina," she starts, hesitating. She looks at Evie, who nods. "I wonder if maybe you're nervous about coming home." She doesn't say anything about how Mina talked to me.

"Maybe," Mina says.

"It's a big step," Evie says. "These feelings of anxiety that you're having are completely normal. I'm glad you're vocalizing them. That's wonderful. Pinehurst is a controlled atmosphere. At home, there are a lot of unknowns. Challenges."

Mom puts a comforting hand on Mina's knee. No one puts their hand on mine.

A hard knot settles in my chest. Evie starts talking about the mountain again. I stop listening. Instead I imagine the cookout happening right now at Hazel's. Hamburgers on the grill. Doing double jumps on her trampoline. Watermelon for dessert.

I look back at Mina, who is now red-faced and fiery. I wish that Evie would ask me again how I think things will be when Mina comes home.

FIRST DAY

I've been to the middle school a few times before—to the auditorium where Mina starred in *Bye Bye Birdie* her eighth-grade year and for the art show where her wire sculpture of a cat won second place. There had also been this day in July where just the incoming sixth graders came in small groups and walked through their schedule and got to eat Rotino's pizza in the cafeteria.

But the halls were quiet then and I was with people I knew: Mom or Mina or the other kids from my elementary school who were feeding into this way bigger school. Nothing could have prepared me for this. Backpacks and back-to-school haircuts and the faint smell of deodorant mixed with the sounds of lockers slamming and people laughing and new sneakers squeaking across the freshly waxed floor.

How do people already have new friends to be laughing with?

I'm trying to find locker number 54 when I spot Hazel.

"Em, Em!" she calls, waving me over. "Oh my gosh. Can you even believe it?" She hooks her arm into mine, pulling me closer. "First day!"

"First day!" I say. Then I look at her outfit. She has on black yoga pants and a shirt that says *PINK* in this purply-plaid writing. "What are you wearing?"

"Isn't it cute?" She smooths down the shirt. Brand new bracelets jingle. They remind me of Gina's.

"I don't remember you sending me that one." I'm trying to think back through all the texts she sent and I'm pretty sure she had decided on this zebra print shirt and jean skirt with her silver earrings.

"Lucy helped me last night."

"Oh." I frown. At the cookout.

"Look!" she says. Hazel's moved on, but I'm still pushing my hands against the fabric of my pants as if I can somehow keep my feelings in. She gestures to her locker like she's showing it off. The inside of it is already decorated. The back of the door is covered with this shiny silver wrapping paper, and she has photos all over it, held in place by little magnets that look like bugs. There's her gerbil, Big Norm, with his miniature party hat from the birthday we threw for him and a magazine cutout of Drew Lewis at the *Undercover Unicorn* premiere. There's the sign I made for her name at summer camp with big bubble letters filled in with thick-markered rainbow stripes.

She pulls one more photo out of her backpack. "It's us," she says. It's eight-year-old us on her front sidewalk, wet from the sprinkler and sticky from our Popsicles. Our smiles are red and blue and big. Our heads and shoulders tilt toward each other as if we're pulled by some invisible magnet.

"Aw, I love that one," I say.

"Hey, I like your shirt," Hazel says, sticking our picture up. "Is it new?"

I smooth down the bottom of it and grin. "Yeah, Mom and I went to the mall—"

"Hazel!" A voice and then arms push me aside, and Hazel's being swallowed up in a hug. "Oh my gosh, you look great." It's Lucy. She's in the same skinny black pants, same T-shirt—only the color is a little different.

Both of them look like they belong under the *New Teen Trends* display.

My clothes suddenly seem all wrong. I cross my arms tightly over my chest.

"I've got to find my locker," I mumble. My sweater is

suddenly itchy and hot, and I need to take it off right this minute.

"Okay!" Hazel says. She's still talking with Lucy. I hear snatches of Lucy's whispers—Joey and his new haircut and the game that weekend. Neither of them notices my tomato-red face. "See you at lunch!"

When I finally find locker 54, the handle jams. I hit the space next to it with my palm.

"You just have to shimmy it," says the girl next to me. "Mine did the same thing." She reaches over, wiggles the handle, and it opens. "Oh, hey! Letter M. Alphabet Girl. Did you finish the book?" Hector's sister. I yank off my sweater and shove it to the very back of the top shelf with my fingertips.

"Whoa." She takes a step back. "That sweater must have done something terrible to you."

"I finished it," I grunt.

"And—"

"And it was good."

"Good?! You mean GREAT, right? That twist at the end with Starlight and Nightshade being long-lost sisters. Amazing! I couldn't even believe it."

"It was pretty cool," I admit. It was actually the best thing. I imagined that maybe Hazel and I could be long-lost sisters, even though it was impossible.

It was nice to pretend.

Anita pulls her planner out of her backpack. It's fancy with a shiny gold glitter cover. She opens it up to the front. "What's your first class?"

I take my schedule from my folder. "Language Arts with Ms. Arnold. Room 203."

"I have Social Studies with Ms. Hohlefelder." She runs her finger down the paper and brightens. "But look, we have Science together fifth period. I'll see you then." She grins.

"Okay," I say. I smile a little, too.

The bell rings, signaling that we have three minutes to get to class. I stand on my tiptoes to see if Hazel's still at her locker, but she's already vanished into the crowd.

When I walk into the classroom, Ms. Arnold is sitting on top of her desk, her legs crossed at the ankles and dangling over the side. On her feet are shoes that look like cats, complete with whiskers and tiny triangle ears.

The bell hasn't rung yet. Lloyd Anderson from last year is already sharpening his pencil, which is no surprise. He stops turning the crank to wave at me. I look away. Marsha Miller's brushing her long straight hair right onto Jimmy Barton's desk, but he's not paying any attention. But that leaves twenty-one stranger faces.

I wind the strap of my backpack around my index finger.

"Let me guess," Ms. Arnold says, running her finger

down her clipboard. "Emily Murphy. Is that right?"

"Em, if that's okay."

Ms. Arnold looks at me closer and I think she's going to tell me no, it's not all right, but instead she says, "I know you!"

"You know me?" I'm not really sure how that's possible. Other teachers "know" me, but that's only because they were here when Mina was and they've accidentally called me her name already this morning. Ms. Arnold's been here only two years I think.

"You were Nightshade!" she says. "At the bookstore. The *Undercover Unicorn* party?"

"You were there?"

"Of course! I haven't missed one yet." She points to a poster at the back of the room. It's the same one I have in my room above my bed: *Nightshade and the Case of the Wandering Wizard.* "You probably don't recognize me, though. I was Ice Apocalypto."

"The snow wizard?"

"Icicles and everything!" It was one thing for me to dress up. But a teacher? That was awesome. The weird breathless feeling that I've been carrying around in my chest all morning starts to fade away. I'm grinning when the bell rings. "You can take a seat right there in the back."

My eyes find the only desk left. It's next to Hector. Soap Boy.

I walk to my new desk slowly and drop my bag on the floor. I slide down into the seat as far as I can, thinking maybe I can disappear. Instead it's just really uncomfortable, so I straighten up and take out my pencils and notebook.

"Oh, cool!" Hector exclaims. He leans over so fast he knocks his textbook off his desk. I hear a few random giggles around us and turn red even though it wasn't me who did anything. "I have that notebook, too." He thrusts his in my direction and he's right. There's an illustration on the front of it with all the Unicorn Chronicles characters together. It has super-fancy spiral binding. Mom bought it for me.

I pretend I don't hear him. Finally Ms. Arnold starts class and I sigh with relief.

I make it to lunchtime. The elementary school cafeteria was set up with skinny rectangular tables—four tables long and four tables wide, with each grade level sitting in a different designated section. But the middle school cafeteria is set up more like a restaurant with round tables that seat eight and booths along the wall. A mural even says *Café* in red cursive, the word flanked by the Eiffel Tower and kids wearing berets. As if it can somehow fool us that we're not in a middle school in the middle of Ohio. But to be honest, it does work a little bit.

I've bought the hot lunch: hot dog, corn chips, and

a scoop of applesauce. There's a little ice cream cup, too. Spumoni, my favorite. I stand on my tiptoes and scan the entire room. A bunch of people brush past me—louder, taller, bigger kids—and I step closer to the wall to get out of the way. Over at the far sides of the cafeteria, I see the back of Hector's head. He's alone at a table. I hope he doesn't turn around. My palms are starting to feel slippery against my tray when I spot Hazel.

She's already at a table with some of her new teammates. I spot Lucy and Annemarie and Gina. Some of the girls look older. I thought we'd just sit with other sixth graders.

"Hazel," I call. Then, I say it a little louder. "Hazel." A few kids chuckle nearby. One nudges his friend and points in my direction. Hazel must hear me, too, because she looks right at me. I hold on to my tray tightly with one hand so I can wave with the other.

"Room for me?" I say when I'm finally close enough not to have to yell anymore. I force myself to sound easy-breezy even though my heart is pounding. As I look around, all the seats are taken. I don't quite know what to do, though, so I just stand there with my tray.

"Sure," Hazel says. She glances at the other girls. "There's room for Em, right? Squeeze in." She scoots over so that she's only occupying half of her chair, and I sit down on the other half—between her and Lucy. I stare at the hot dog on my tray like it's the most interesting thing ever and try to ignore the fact that Lucy has scooted her lunch all the way over so that it doesn't touch mine.

"You'll never guess who I'm sitting by in Language Arts," I whisper. "The ogre!"

"Who?" Lucy asks. She takes a bite of salad from her Tupperware container. I look around. I'm the only one who has a hot lunch. Everyone else brought one from home.

"You know, Hector. Soap Boy." I wince the second I say it and glance over to where he's sitting like maybe he heard me, even though there's no way. He's not alone now, though. Ms. Arnold has her hand on his table and is laughing. Maybe they're talking about Nightshade. I'm brought back by a pinch on my leg, and I know I've said the wrong thing. Lucy's giving Hazel a raised-eyebrow look.

"What?" I rush out. "Someone called him that in class. Is that not his name?"

"That's the worst," Lucy says, making a face. "Did he smell?"

I nod. It isn't a lie, but I actually thought he smelled kind of pleasant—like mint toothpaste and pancakes. Lucy shakes her head like she knew it all along.

I'm quiet after that. I don't want to say anything else wrong, so I just listen. There's a bunch of "Did you see's" and "Did you hear's" and whether or not they'd have to run laps at practice later. I'm thinking to myself as I take a bite of applesauce that I could do this. I could sit next to Hazel for the next couple of months and just keep to myself and to my food. And if someone's glance would fall on the table for a quick second, it might look like I actually belong.

That's sounding pretty good to me as I move on to my chips when I feel a hand on my shoulder. I look up.

It's a man with a mustache and a whistle and a giant yellow stain on his tie where he probably tried to wipe off a blob of mustard. "You can't sit here," he says to me. "It's a fire hazard. One student per seat." The other girls look anywhere but me. My heart's in my throat now and I can't seem to speak.

I nod and grab my tray. I worry that my trembly legs won't be able to hold me up.

"Ugh, he's so unfair," Hazel says when the teacher walks away. She doesn't get up. "What's the worst that can happen, you know? Like there's really going to be some fire."

"We could sit over there," I say. I nudge Hazel's shoulder with my tray because it doesn't seem like she's heard me. She's taking a carrot stick off Lucy's napkin.

"Oh, what?" Hazel looks where I'm pointing. There's this little booth that has a few crumpled napkins on top of it, but it's empty and we'll fit.

"Sure," Hazel says slowly. She moves to stand.

"Nooo. Staayy!" Lucy says.

"Yeah, don't go, Hazel," Annemarie chimes in. "We have

very important team stuff to talk about."

Another two of the older girls giggle. Only Gina looks a little bit guilty.

Hazel makes a frown face. "Tomorrow, okay?" She holds out her pinky for me to shake.

It's a good thing that our bodies do a lot of things automatically—our hearts beat, our lungs breathe—because in that moment my feet somehow start walking on their own. So instead of being the weirdo girl standing in the middle of the cafeteria where everyone can see her, I'm the weirdo girl sitting in a little booth all by myself.

Ms. Arnold has moved on from Hector's table now and is patrolling the aisleways with her clipboard. I see her stop and watch me slip out of sight. I will her not to come over. The only thing worse than sitting alone is sitting with the teacher who feels sorry for you.

I tuck myself right against the wall on the side, facing away from the girls. But I can't get away from Hazel's laughter that cuts clear across the room. It's this goose honking sound, but from her it sounds quirky and charming.

I resist the urge to turn around and look over my shoulder. Instead, I take a bite out of my hot dog. It's ketchup-less and cold.

GIANT NEON ARROW

On the Saturday after Dad left for good, we ran out for groceries and came back with a dog. Mina suggested we make sandwiches with thick bacon and tomato and lettuce, as if that would somehow fix everything.

It was Mina who first spotted Bean. She was two stores down from the grocery at the pet food store in the same plaza. People had set up lawn chairs and a table out front. There was a sign, *Columbus Greyhound Rescue*, and a bunch of skinny dogs lined up on leashes wearing bright knitted sweaters.

Mina took me and Mom by the hands and dragged us both over. One named Princess Cupcake shoved her nose up on Mina's knee, right where her jeans had split. "This is the one," Mina said.

I guess if Dad could meet someone new, then so could we.

I studied her. Long spindly legs, narrow nose. She tilted her head to the side like she was waiting for me to say something. "She looks like a bean," I said. She did. One of the long fancy green beans that Grandma Bebe would serve on our Thanksgiving plates with almonds and butter. The name stuck.

Bean wasn't used to being in a home. All she knew was the track and her kennel. Everything was brand new to her: the way our couch sank in the middle, the slipperiness of the floor, her reflection in the mirror. We had to walk her around the house on a leash. Mark the windows and the individual panes of glass door with blue painter's tape so she wouldn't crash through them. Teach her how to take the steps one at a time. Show her where to go outside and what things were okay to lie on.

That's what I needed.

Not so much the tape and everything—I wasn't going to bust through any middle school windows by accident—but a guide. Instructions. Advice. Somehow, everyone seems to know what to do—who to laugh with, how to bring their lunch, where to sit—but me.

That's what I'm thinking about at midnight. I can't sleep.

My T-shirt blanket, which normally feels cozy, only feels scratchy on my legs, and the little fan on my dresser isn't enough to cool me off. Even Bean is restless and flops her little body from side to side every five minutes or so.

I need to stop thinking about everything that's happened the past few days. Between Mina coming home soon and my back-to-school outfit and lunchtime and getting a permanent seat next to Soap Boy, my insides feel all shaken up like a snow globe. The little pieces refuse to settle.

I do all the normal things I do when I can't sleep. First, I pull my calendar off the wall. I count. There's five days till Mina comes home. Thirty-six days till the Unicorn Chronicles movie premiere. A hundred and seventy-nine school days till the end of sixth grade. Ugh. That is forever. Thinking about it only makes it harder to get back to sleep.

I write and delete text messages to Hazel:

Emily: Sra. Alvarez says dog in Spanish is perro. Bean es un perro. Cool, right?
Emily: How was practice tonight? What was the important team stuff?
Emily: Why didn't you sit with me?

Then I reread the end of *Moaning Moat*. I've had it for only a few days, but I've already read the whole thing twice and dog-eared the pages. Even though Hazel told me not to read the end first, I totally did. Knowing how something ends makes it a lot easier to enjoy what it takes to get there, I think.

But Nightshade's adventures aren't enough to distract me. I shift Bean off my leg, throw my blanket to the side, and scoot off the bed. My feet are quiet against the floor and even Bean seems to have gotten the message, because when she jumps, she lands on my giant floor pillow instead of the hardwood.

I open up my bedroom door, making sure it doesn't creak and wake Mom.

Downstairs, I pour myself Cinnamon Toast Crunch and milk. I make a little bowl of kibble for Bean.

We flop down on the couch and Bean burrows in next to me. She breathes warm little puffs onto my arm. I rub her ear a little; it's like velvet. She loves that. With the other hand, I flip the TV on with the remote and cycle through the channels. *I Love Lucy* reruns, a religious show with some old lady talking about salvation, late night talk. Finally, I find what I'm looking for.

Infomercials.

Hazel doesn't get it. She always makes me turn them off at sleepovers, saying, "Emily, it's just like a long commercial. We can skip over those." But I like them. Some of the stuff is really cool and practical: a blanket with sleeves, a knife that can cut through shoes, a small towel that can wipe up huge gallon-sized messes. And not only that, but the people on the infomercials are smiley and enthusiastic in spite of their inability to do anything right. That might be why I like them best of all. There is possibility in it—that someone could do so many wrong things but still come out the other side happy.

I sit back, expecting to see some kind of magical blender or mighty putty, but some guy comes on who I've never seen before.

"Hello there," he says.

His voice is calm. "Have you had a bad day?" At this, I almost choke on a cereal square. Bean pops her head up and looks at me, concerned.

I cough a couple of times, then whisper, "I'm okay." She doesn't look convinced, so I set down my spoon and cereal bowl and pat the little bald spot on the top of her head.

The man continues. "Maybe you've had a bad month or a bad year. Maybe your life seems a little bit out of control." At this, I lean forward. It's strange, but it's like he is talking directly to me. "Do you need a guide to help you face your problems head-on? A pathway to a new and improved YOU?"

This is it. A sign. A giant neon arrow pointing at the TV.

Yes. Yes!

The camera pans back to show the man now sitting in an armchair. It has an old-fashioned paisley pattern, and there's a cat on his lap. "If you answered yes to any of these questions, I have a solution for you. Introducing the *Be the Best You* series from Mind over Matter Industries. This series of CDs specially created by me, Dr. Henry Franklinton-Morehouse, will allow you to discover the best you. A you that's capable of being in control and not only facing your problems but solving them."

That all sounds great to me.

"Each of our CDs will focus on the *Be the Best You* principles and will include different exercises to help you incorporate them into your own life. The program has been successfully implemented again and again in a series of studies we've conducted. Meet Marlena."

Now there's a lady with headphones on. She's sitting at a kitchen table. Every few seconds or so, she nods thoughtfully and jots something down in a notebook. "Marlena was just like you. Lost. Confused. Without direction."

At this, Marlena takes off the headphones and turns toward the camera. "But then I found the *Be the Best You* CDs and they changed my life. My marriage was in trouble. My aunt was sick. I found it hard to deal with everyday problems. But these CDs changed my thinking. They turned my

I Can'ts into I Cans. I found a new job. I sought out travel and new situations. I grew better at taking chances. I truly did become a better me. A new me."

I lean back against the couch, and my heart is bouncing in my chest. Marlena's life kind of does sound like mine. Mom and Dad are broken up. Mina's sick. I don't need a new job, but I do want to make it through sixth grade, and right now that seems like a lot of work.

Now Dr. Henry Franklinton-Morehouse is back on. "If you want your life changed like Marlena's, don't hesitate. Call now for a very special offer. The first twenty callers will get the *Be the Best You* CD set for the low price of forty dollars."

I turn to Bean. "This could be the answer!" I jump from the couch and race up the stairs as quietly as I can. I lift up the right-hand corner of my mattress and feel around until my hand finds the little tear in the fabric. I wiggle my fingers in and pull out a small roll of bills I saved up from weeding Mrs. Pruett's garden this summer.

With a leap down the hall and an excited tiptoe down the stairs, I'm back to a waiting Bean. I sit on the floor and count out the money while she watches. "One, two, three," I whisper, smoothing out each of the bills. When I get to the last dollar, I shake my head. "Twenty-two dollars, Bean. It's not enough."

I start to stack up the money when I get a thought. It's a pretty bad thought. But at the same time, really pretty good. Right next to the number on the bottom of the screen are different payment options.

And one of those options is a credit card.

Mom has a credit card. It's for emergencies only, she says, but what is this situation if not an emergency?

Mom's wallet is on the counter, not even in her purse or anything. I open it but pause when I see the unopened stack of bills from the mail earlier. I should just ask Mom if it's okay.

But she doesn't need one more thing to worry about. Besides, in the hierarchy of worry, with Mina at the top and then the stuff with Dad and then the bills and her job and paying for Mina's treatment, which is "not cheap," my problems fall at the very bottom. I try to ignore the little pang of guilt in my stomach and pull the card out of its slot. Bean's watching me.

I take a deep breath and pick up the phone. It's old and still attached to its cradle by a springy cord. "It works fine," Mom said whenever Mina asked about getting a different one. And it does work fine as I pull the cord around into the family room. I carefully punch in the numbers on the screen and take a deep breath.

It rings once. Twice.

"Good evening," a voice says.

"Um, hi," I reply. For all this watching of infomercials, I'm not really sure how the whole process of ordering works. "Is this Dr. Henry Franklinton-Morehouse?"

The voice laughs. "No, this is Dave from the call center. Would you like to be the best you YOU can be?" He's enthusiastic, like some self-help cheerleader.

I nod, even though Dave from the call center can't see me. "Yes, I'd like that very much."

"Well, you made the right call," he says.

I say my name is Maura Murphy. I read the numbers off the front of the card just like Mom does when she orders pizza (which Mom classifies as a dinner emergency). I flip the card over and read the three special numbers on the back.

It's easy. It's the first easy thing that's happened today.

To be honest, now I'm kind of worried about myself because here I am stealing and then lying to this nice man on the phone.

Just like that, it's done and Dave says, "Okay, we'll ship the CDs out to you at the address you've provided. They'll be there in five to seven business days."

Five to seven days?! I calculate the time in my head. That means they'll get here *maybe* next Friday. It seems like a very long time to wait. "Can they get here any faster?"

"Would you like to add expedited shipping?"

I grimace. Shipping things faster always costs extra money. Money that I don't really have, but I can't make myself say no. Instead I say, "Yes, that would be great. Thank you. The faster the better."

I hear the clicking of the computer keys in the background and then Dave says, "Okay, you're all set. They'll go out right away. You must really need these CDs!"

Dave doesn't know the half of it.

WILDEBEESTS

The next day, Mom drops me off at school early. She has to open the bank today.

The parking lot is empty except for a few cars and teachers toting giant bags and steaming cups of coffee.

"Coffee," Mom says in one long breath. "That's what I forgot. I don't even know how I'm functioning right now." She leans over and gives me a kiss on the cheek. "I put a Honey Bun in your lunch bag for breakfast."

I had packed my own lunch today.

When Mom had gone to pull the peanut butter and jelly out of the cupboard, I had asked, "Could I have a salad instead?"

Mom turned around, her eyebrows knit together. "You don't even like vegetables."

I shrugged. I was propped up on a stool at the kitchen counter. "I don't know," I said. "Giving something new a try, I guess."

Mom grabbed the bagged salad out of the fridge, a Tupperware container, and a lunch tote. "Okay, honey," Mom said. "It's great to try different things." She paused. Her next words were slow, careful. "You're not having bad thoughts, right? About food?"

I rolled my eyes. "Mom. I just want some vegetables. I'm not Mina." Even my own lunch has to be about her.

Mom sighed. "I know." She paused. "But you're not having bad thoughts?"

"No! Other parents would be thrilled. It's salad!" I don't really want salad. But literally the last thing Mom needs is me telling her about lunchroom drama. "Could I have it in a brown bag, too?" I hopped down and rustled through the drawers. There had to be one somewhere. "It's just easier. I don't have to go back to my locker after lunch to put anything away."

My story seemed to work.

"Thanks, Mom," I say. I close the car door and wave as she drives away. The paper bag makes a satisfying crinkle in my fist. It's a reminder that today will be better.

The school's different this time of day. The hallways are quiet except for the squeaks of my sneakers. The floor's clean—free from outside recess shoe prints and crumpled pieces of looseleaf. The lights are even softer. There's not the harsh fluorescent glare of the daytime.

It's so much easier to breathe right now.

At my locker, I sit on the floor. I take out my napkin and open the Honey Bun package. Then I pull out the decorations I packed up last night. Leftover polka-dot wrapping paper. A drawing of Bean. A little mirror I found in the bathroom drawer. The picture of me and Hazel from before the bookstore party.

I jiggle the handle the way Anita showed me yesterday. The door opens right away. I should have said thank you. It's a good trick.

I'm taking a bite of my breakfast and trying to figure how to fit the paper on the inside of my locker, when I hear the *click-clack* of heels on the linoleum. They're getting louder. I turn and there's Ms. Arnold with a stack of papers in one arm. I turn. She stops.

"Good morning!" She smiles. Today, she's wearing a gray skirt and this fuchsia sweater with sequins. I wonder, for a second, if it would be weird to ask her for clothing advice. I decide against it. "You're here early."

"My mom had to work," I say, after I finish chewing. "I'm

decorating my locker." I think back to the cafeteria yesterday and the one-person-one-seat rule. A pit of worry settles in my stomach. "I'm allowed to be here, right?"

"Of course," Ms. Arnold says. "Decorate away!" She takes a step, then thinks better of it. "You know, Em, I'm glad I ran into you. There's actually this thing I'm thinking of starting. Once a week, before school starts. Like a club."

"What kind of club?"

"It doesn't have a name yet," she says. "But we'll play games. Talk. Maybe about books." She winks at me. "A very low-key club. Not a lot of rules."

It does kind of sound like fun. Maybe better than sitting in an empty hallway. It's not like I can decorate my locker every day. "Who's in it?"

"I think Sara Miller," she says. I try to picture Sara. She sits in the back of Science and has the cool beads on the end of her braids that clink together when she turns her head. "Lloyd Anderson. Hector Garcia . . ."

Hazel's voice pops into my head. *Hector Garcia. Soap Boy. A name you don't want.* I think of sitting alone at lunch and the CDs that will be delivered that afternoon that will fix everything. I'm not quite sure who brand new Em is, but I'm thinking she doesn't play games with the teacher and Hector Garcia before school. The goal is to be a Better Me, not a Weirder Me.

I try to think fast. "That sounds cool," I say. I wrap the edge of my T-shirt around my finger. "But I don't think I can. My mom's schedule changes a lot."

"I understand," she says. "But know that the invitation's out there. Okay?"

"Scientists," Mrs. Judd says to start class. She doesn't call us boys and girls or ladies and gentlemen or even "you guys" like some teachers. She always calls us scientists. I like it; it sounds more official. "Migration is based on necessity."

She has the lights off and the Smart Board screen turned on. On it is an image of a bird taking flight. I'm in the back of the classroom between Sara and Anita, but the picture's big and bright and I can see it clearly. It looks so real I wouldn't be surprised if I felt the air from its wings on the top of my head.

"When you hear the word migration, you first think of birds and flying south for the winter. Why do they do this?"

Sara raises her hand. Mrs. Judd nods in her direction. "Warmer climate?" she says.

"In part, yes. But even more importantly, they're in search of food. If they have enough food in one place, they might put off migration. They do what it takes to stay alive."

She clicks the presenter button. A new picture fills the screen. It's a big brown animal with black zebra stripes and a furry beard under its chin. "This is the wildebeest. These animals travel over eighteen hundred miles a year in search of water and food. And this is not without peril."

She clicks onto another slide. There's a wildebeest in the water in the jaws of crocodile.

Joey Peters nudges the kid next to him and laughs. "What a dumb animal," he calls out. I see Anita roll her eyes from where I'm sitting.

"There's nothing funny about survival, Mr. Peters," Mrs. Judd says. "And I'd think twice before laughing about the wildebeest. One, they're big animals who run very, very fast."

"They'd crush him," Sara whispers. It's unexpected coming from her. I glance over at her notes. In the margin she's sketched a miniature wildebeest racing after a flailing Joey, his ball cap flying off his head. I hide a smile behind my hand. She sees me looking and grins.

"Two, they use something called swarm intelligence. They cooperate with each other. They have a common goal and work together to achieve it. Crossing rivers, avoiding predators like lions and cheetahs, protecting the young. As a group. Very smart, I think."

Mrs. Judd switches to an aerial picture of them, taken high in the sky. The wildebeests look small now, like specks of pepper spilled out from the shaker. There are hundreds, maybe thousands of them, all moving the same direction.

"Together," she says, "their odds of survival are much greater than if they were alone."

When the bell rings for lunchtime, I hurry to my locker to grab my lunch and then race to the cafeteria. I'll wait for Hazel outside it so I'm not last to the table again.

To be honest, it's kind of a dangerous place to be. Two eighth graders are jostling, and one almost knocks the other into me. I'm nearly run over by a cart of clean hot-lunch trays. By the time Hazel arrives, my knuckles have turned bright white from gripping my lunch bag so hard.

"Hey!" I say, linking my arm with hers. Each of us part of an Em-Hazel arm pretzel. "I have to show you my locker later. I got this great polka-dotted paper. And I put our picture—" I glance at her. She's on her tiptoes, looking out over everyone. "Earth to Hazel." Hazel's only half listening. I wave my hand in front of her face.

"Oh, sorry." She turns to me and gives me a small smile. "Polka-dotted paper. Awesome. Where do you want to sit today?"

"I don't know. How about that table over there?"

"Sure, okay."

The table is tucked up against the wall so that the first chair faces the direction of the mural and the other faces out to the cafeteria. Hazel takes the second one.

I unpack my salad and fork. I spear one of the pieces of lettuce and make a face. This sounded like a very good idea last night and not so much of a great idea right now. I chew. It tastes like eating ranch-flavored grass.

Hazel pulls out her salad, too, and she's just munching away like she's a regular old rabbit. I never knew she liked salad so much.

"Cute pants," she says.

I smooth my hands over the top of them. They're jeans. Not the stretchy leggings material Hazel and Lucy wore yesterday. But they're black and skinny. Similar, I think. I'm trying to do the *right things* today. Though now Hazel and the other girls are wearing their ERMS field hockey half-zips with their last names and numbers on the back. I don't have one of those.

I'm getting the feeling that middle school is like this giant footrace and I'm always three or four steps behind.

"Hey, so about the movie—"

Hazel interrupts me. "Oh my gosh." Her eyebrows shoot up. "I almost forgot to tell you. Guess who I sit by in Spanish?" She leans forward, closing the gap between us.

"Who? Lucy?"

"No! Joey Peters!" she exclaims. I think about Joey in Science class and his dumb jokes.

"Can you even believe it? Well, okay, he's actually like

four seats away. But that's pretty close. And today when he got up to talk to Señora Alvarez, his sneaker touched mine." My head tilts. Hazel sounds so excited about it.

I put the lid on the rest of my salad and stuff it into my bag. I don't want to have any more. "Was your foot in the way?"

"Em, no!" She taps my arm with the back of her fork. "It was a sign. You know." She's smiling now, this little secret kind of smile.

"A sign?" I wait for her to go on.

"I dunno! Like I'm special. Maybe he's thinking of me." Her cheeks are flushed red now like she's just come in from the cold. "Can you even believe it? He is super *muy linda*. That means cute, right? Soo cute."

"That's great," I say. I try to sound excited, but I'm still thinking about Nightshade and the movie and making plans. "So, do you want to—"

"I've *got* to tell Lucy. Be right back, okay?"

She starts striding over to the snack bar, throwing looks in the direction of Lucy's table. Lucy sees her and their brainwaves must be in sync, because she pops right out of her seat and joins her in line. Suddenly, I'm the girl sitting alone again.

I know Hazel's telling her the story because she touches Lucy's shoe with her own, acting the whole thing out. Lucy grabs her arms then and they squeal together. Deep in my stomach, there's a knowing. That's what I should have done. When Hazel told me, I should have reached over the table and grabbed her hand and squeezed it tight. We should have chair danced in celebration.

The bell rings to signal the end of lunch. Hazel's spent more time in the snack line than she did with me.

"Em, sorry!" she says, trying to dodge around all the kids who are now exiting the cafeteria to make it back to our table. She has half a chocolate chip cookie in her hand—the good gooey kind that is a little soft in the middle. My stomach rumbles. All I've had is a bite or two of salad. "Lucy says she's going to try to find a bigger table. So we can all sit together tomorrow. Isn't that cool of her?"

"Yeah, that's great." Inside, though, my heart twists. What's so wrong with just me and Hazel? Am I not enough?

I look over at Lucy. In her hand is the other half of Hazel's cookie.

BE THE BEST ME!

When I get home from school that afternoon, there's a package on our front porch, shimmied right under our doormat.

"Yes!" I cheer out loud, dancing the little victory jig Hazel and I invented for occasions such as this. In one motion, I grab it off the porch and unlock the door with my key.

"They're here, they're here," I yell upstairs. Bean's head appears at the top and then she *thump-thumps* down the steps.

In that moment, I'm the bean. A jumping bean, and I can hardly still my arms and leg. I grab a scissors from the kitchen and slice open the packing tape. I open the box.

There's a large CD case inside with Dr. Henry Franklinton-Morehouse's picture on the front. He just looks so smart, and I bet if that picture could talk he'd say, "Today's your day, Emily Murphy. Today's the day you become a better you."

I gather up the packaging and stuff it in the outside trash can. Hiding the evidence, I guess. Now I need to find a CD player. I really wish I could have just downloaded it on iTunes, but maybe really good wisdom has to be communicated in a different way.

"Do we have a CD player, Bean?" She just wags her tail.

I'm squinting my eyes shut and thinking, thinking, thinking, when suddenly an image of seventh-grade Mina pops into my mind. She's dancing around her room, preparing for the schoolwide talent show, headphones on, *listening to a portable CD player.*

"Mina has one!"

I charge up the stairs and burst into her room.

I'm trying to think of where it could be. First, I look under her bed—just a bunch of her magazines I've already read and some old papers she wrote for English class. Then I look in her closet. Clothes she didn't bring with her to Pinehurst because they were now too big swing on the hangers. I open the tubs of shoes and purses that sit on the floor. I find a random knickknack or souvenir wedged in but no CD player. My mind goes to the drawer at the top of her dresser where she keeps a whole bunch of stuff that doesn't quite fit anywhere else. I bet it's there.

I run across the room and open it.

I riffle through yarn from a scarf she had started knitting for Bean, a bunch of loose pictures, old school supplies. No CD player. But then I see something else. Small and red, large wire spirals on the side. I swallow hard and open the notebook up. Mina's small, neat handwriting fills the pages. Inky blue reminders of last winter.

December 18—Breakfast: grapes, water
Lunch: Jell-O (sugar free)
Exercise: 100 sit-ups, running

I close it with a sharp snap. My fingers tingle, and I practically throw it back in the drawer and bury it as deep as I can.

That notebook is from the past.

I take a deep breath. Mina leaving happened to Before Emily. Right now I'm working on Future Em. Future Em can handle anything—Mina and Dad and sixth grade. I find the CD player and headphones, grab them out of the drawer, and close Mina's door behind me.

Back in my room, I take some batteries out of my top desk drawer and pop them into the player. I rip a few sheets of loose leaf out of a notebook and sit down with my official Unicorn Chronicles special-edition pencil.

I am ready to be the Best Me Ever!

I hit play. As I wait for the CD player to whir to life, I write *BE A BETTER ME!!!* in gigantic letters at the top of the paper. Then, gentle music begins. It sounds like what you might hear in a department store elevator. Finally, there's a voice. It's deep and low. "I'm Dr. Henry Franklinton-Morehouse. Welcome to the *Be the Better You* audio series. Just by the very step of you purchasing these CDs from our Mind over Matter Industries, you have shown yourself to be committed to the act of self-improvement. Congratulations!"

I find myself wondering if he's taping this from the paisley chair in the infomercial, but I refocus. "There are five steps to becoming a better you. Each lesson will focus on a different step. First, though, we need to get a baseline. Just like those wardrobe makeover shows on TV, you won't know how dramatic the new you is unless you examine who you are now."

Dramatic. Yes! I won't even recognize the old me.

"We won't be showing your photos side by side, though. No, your change will come from within. Take a piece of paper and a pencil. Good. Now draw a giant lowercase *T* in the center. On the left side of the *T*, at the very top, I want you to write *Before Me.* On the right side I want you to write

After Me. We'll concentrate on the left side for now."

I divide my paper like he says. I write *Before Emily* on one side and *After Emily* on the other.

"Now write words that describe you at this point in your life. To get your brain going, start with the easy stuff. Your name, maybe. Or your age. That will get you warmed up." Music starts playing again—birds and a babbling brook and whistling wind. Thinking music.

Hmm. Things I know about me.

~~Emily~~ Em Murphy
Almost twelve.
Sixth grader.
Hazel's best friend.

Dr. Franklinton-Morehouse comes on again. "Okay, now for the harder stuff. Who are you inside? I want you to picture your backyard. What do you see? Grass, dirt. Maybe some flowers. Now take a shovel. Dig a hole. What do you find? Wormholes, rocks, tiny bugs. That's what I want you to do now. Look beyond the surface of who you are."

I tap the eraser end of my pencil against the desk. I think Dr. Franklinton-Morehouse wants character traits, like the ones we have to pick out in Language Arts class about different book characters. For example, Nightshade. Hers are super easy to come up with. She's brave, heroic, brilliant, a great friend.

But who am I? I squeeze my eyes shut to think harder.

Likes unicorn detectives. True, but everyone knows that.

I think about Mina and how far away she sat on the couch. *Bad sister.* The backs of my eyes start to tingle.

Bad daughter. Dad left. Mina left.

I click stop on the CD player. I look at the list I have. To be honest, it's kind of depressing.

FIVE THOUSAND PIECES

When I go downstairs, I see that Mom's home. She has on her old jeans and her hair's pulled up into a messy ponytail with a regular old rubber band. Her cleaning clothes. She's carrying a toaster to the front door, where there's already a pile of junk growing: old toy dolls from when me and Mina were younger, my beginning ballet dance tutu, a rusted trike that's hung out in the back of our basement. I pick one of the dolls up from the pile. There are still traces of the bright red lipstick Mina and I smeared on her eyebrows when we gave her a makeover.

"You sure were quiet up there," she says. "I peeked in but didn't want to interrupt. Homework?"

"Something like that," I say, glad I didn't leave the packaging for the CDs where she could find it. "What are you doing?"

Mom shakes open a black trash bag. "Spring cleaning. Or fall cleaning, I should say. We just have so much junk. I thought it would be good to get some of that out of here. Organized house, organized mind—they say."

"Who says that?"

Mom shakes her head at the pile and laughs. "Not anyone in this house. But maybe we could try. Want to help me bring a few more things up from the basement?"

All I really want to do is listen to the next portion of the CDs. Now that I have an idea of who I am, how do I become better? But Mom has this kind of hopeful look on her face—like the one Bean has when she thinks she's getting a dog bone. "Okay, sure."

Together, we go downstairs. The basement's like this weird messy museum of our family. There are shelves and shelves of broken dolls, camping gear, Mina's old trophies, a vintage bowling ball collection (which is maybe the weirdest). Mom's already started to organize. There are three piles on the floor. "This one's the throw-away. This one's to donate, and this stuff we've got to find a new home for." The last pile is the biggest one. "Why don't you go through the stuff on those shelves over there."

I kneel down and look at the bottom shelf. There's a bunch of Mina's stuff on it. "Okay, what about this little microphone thing?" I hold it up so Mom can take a look. There's an attachment where you can hook it into the TV. Mina used to perform mini concerts for her stuffed animals.

"Keep, probably," Mom says, even though it's super unlikely that Mina will ever use it again.

"Stuffed alligator?" One of his eyes is torn off and his tail is dyed a strange shade of blue. Probably exploded Magic Marker.

"Keep again," Mom says. "You know, go ahead and move onto the next shelf. We probably should wait till she gets home to make any decisions about her stuff." There's a pause, and I know what's coming next. "How are you feeling about that?"

"About waiting till she gets home? Smart. We wouldn't want to accidentally throw away this dumb alligator." I toss it back onto the shelf.

"Emily," Mom warns. Then she softens. "About her coming home. I know things were hard before and—"

"No, it's good. I'm excited. Golf club?" I hold it in the air.

Mom sighs her very biggest sigh. "Pitch." The golf club was Dad's.

"Old pair of shoes." They still had mud on them from when Dad took us hiking.

"Pitch."

"You know, Emily—it's okay to talk about things."

"I know. That's what Wednesdays are for." I'm feeling a little huffy now. I came down here to clean and throw things out and now I'm being trapped into some kind of unexpected Feelings Conversation. I've said what I'm supposed to say and now I want to move on.

"Puzzle?" I pull the box from the back of the shelf. The cardboard pieces rattle.

There's another sigh again. Sometimes it seems like that's all Mom does. "What does it look like?"

I turn it over in my hands so the picture faces front. "Map of the world. There's a bunch of animals and monuments and stuff."

Mom comes over. I hand it to her. "Talk about a blast from the past," she says. "Wow. I hadn't thought about this in forever." There's a small smile on her face. "You know, when your Dad and I were first married, we didn't have tons of money, so we'd do a puzzle on the weekends."

I try to picture younger Dad and younger Mom—the ones I've seen in pictures: Dad with an easy smile and goofy mustache and Mom with long blond hair around a table. Smiling. Happy. Together. I mean, I read books about unicorn detectives. But somehow this seems way harder to imagine.

"Fun, Mom," I say, even though it's the furthest possible thing from fun.

Mom swats my arm with the box. "They were fun. Your mom is totally fun. Hey, what do you think about us doing one of these together?"

"It's five thousand pieces."

"And? You have to be somewhere? You'd rather clean?" She gestures around to the basement, most of which we haven't tackled.

I shrug. "Sure, then. We can do a puzzle."

She hands me the box. "You put a smile on that face and take this upstairs. I'll bring up the card table. We'll need somewhere to set it up."

I start for the steps. "Where do you want it?"

There's a long pause before she says anything back. "What about the dining room? It seems silly that it's still empty, doesn't it?"

My answer comes out small. "Okay."

I get to the top of the steps and look at the dining room off to the left. There's an old-fashioned rolling door with rectangular wooden panels of different colors decorating it like a checkerboard. It's kind of odd, but Mom always liked it and said that's the really great thing about old houses: they have "character."

I grab onto the brass handle and roll back the door. It mumbles and groans. The hinges creak. Mom used to oil them. Bean barks from upstairs like she does anytime she doesn't recognize a sound.

"It's okay, Bean," I call up. I say it as much for me as for her.

I flip the switch on the wall. The light flicks on and the ceiling fan comes to life. It swirls the dust around like they're tiny pieces of snow. Unlike Mina's room, Mom hasn't cleaned in here in a long time. There wasn't a reason to. Dad's not coming back.

But here we are.

Two fancy silver candlesticks sit tarnished in the corner. Every year for my birthday, Mom would get out the good china and the goblets of sparkling grape juice. She'd light the candles and they'd give off this cozy glow and make the room feel like something special. I'd get to invite a friend. I always asked Hazel. And we'd sit there—me, Mom, Dad, Mina, and Hazel eating pot roast and fluffy rolls with butter and chocolate cake for dessert. My favorite.

Everything's so different now.

Mom joins me at the door. She's holding the card table and also looks a little bit like she's going to cry.

"Okay!" I say, shaking my head as if it will make the

bad feelings disappear, like some kind of imaginary Etch A Sketch. I make it a point not to look at Mom too long. I don't want to remember the twisty crying face she had as she'd sit in front of the TV in the days after Dad left. "It's a sad movie," she'd tell us, even though she had just been watching some game show or something. "It's a sad commercial," she'd tell me once Mina had gone.

"Let's set this up," I say. I take the table from Mom and unfold the legs so that they click into place. I turn the table right side up. Mom drags in two chairs from the kitchen table. I sit in one and fold my left leg under my body.

Bean noses on into the room and starts sniffing around the corners and edges of the walls. There are a lot of unfamiliar smells for her.

Mom takes a deep breath. I can tell she's remembering—her and Dad. Or maybe all of us in this room where we used to celebrate holidays together. Then she dumps out the pieces. "Okay, puzzle strategy."

"Strategy? I always thought you kind of just put them together."

"Emily, no." Mom looks like I've personally wounded her. "I feel like I've failed you as a mother. We have to flip all the pieces over first." She starts flipping them all to the colorful illustration side. "Then we have pick out all the edge pieces. And then sort them by color. There's a system." She stands the top of the box up so we have the picture to help us.

We sit there for I don't know how long. Maybe an hour. Maybe more. Mom says Puzzle Time is like magic because it passes by so quickly. She said she and Dad would sometimes just have popcorn dinner instead of real dinner so they could keep working.

The candles still sit in the corner, but tonight in there with Mom kind of feels cozy and warm in its own way.

Mom goes to heat us up some macaroni and cheese. I take a picture of the progress we've made so far and text it to Hazel. It's not a lot. We've just put together the lower half of Africa. There's a roaring lion and some grasslands and a bit of the ocean. But it actually is kind of cool—Mom was right.

Emily: 48367 pieces to go! :P Maybe you can help us.

I wait for a response, but the minutes go by. Nothing.

Bean turns belly up so I can give her a rub. I take a picture of her face and try again.

Emily: Upside-down dog!

Hazel loves Googling pictures of upside-down dogs. Their faces look so goofy. She still doesn't text me back. The uneasy feeling from today in the cafeteria returns.

When I go upstairs for bed, I pull out my list to add two things. First, I write *good-ish at puzzles.* Then I write a question mark next to *Hazel's best friend.*

DAD'S HOUSE

Mom drops me off at Dad's house Saturday afternoon after she gets home from work.

Dad's house is nothing like our house, which is cozy and small with lots of rooms. Dad's house is big and blocky and so brand-new it doesn't even have grass yet. It just has a big, yard-sized rectangle of dirt.

It's the kind of neighborhood where all the mailboxes are the same. Different from our neighborhood, where mailboxes are all different shapes and colors. One is even the shape of a duck. Interesting, not boring.

Alice greets me at the door with Pickle meowing like crazy under one arm. She waves at Mom's car like they're old friends and not like she's Dad's new person. My heart hurts when I watch her drive away because I know Mom's going home alone. She has Bean to keep her company, but that's not quite the same.

"Emily! Come in," she says. She reaches for my sleeping bag and pillow, but I hold on to them in front of me like a shield. She eyes them. "We have a bed for you, you know."

"I know," I say.

If Alice were anyone but Alice, I'd probably like her. She has these funky glasses and knows a lot about TV game shows and has actually read all the Unicorn Chronicles books like me and Mina. That's usually such a good way to judge someone's character.

I wait for a Mina question. People who know about Mina always ask about her first. But there, standing in the front hallway on their brand-new fancy rug, she says, "How are you?" She reaches out to touch my hand.

How am I? A lump forms in my throat. "Fine," I say. I shift my duffel bag from one hand to the other. It's so light. I've barely packed anything at all. "I'm going to take my stuff upstairs."

"Okay, yeah. Great!" Alice grins. She's not bothered by my not wanting to talk. Or maybe she's just good at covering her feelings up. "Your dad should be home soon. He thought we could go bowling tonight. Won't that be fun?"

I like bowling. The sound of the ball hitting the pins, the glow-in-the-dark lane lines, the cheese fries sprinkled with bacon. But I don't like that Dad suggested it. I shrug.

Alice's grin fades a little. "There are some paint samples on your dresser, too. Maybe take a look and see if there's one you like. I'd love to get going on your room."

I'm almost all the way up the steps when Alice calls my name. "Yeah?" I say and turn around.

"I'm glad you're here," she replies.

When Dad first told me about the new house he said, "There's lots of room!" like it was some kind of huge selling point. He even stretched out his arms as if to somehow demonstrate exactly how much room there would be. I didn't know why he needed so much space when there was just Dad, Alice, Pickle, and sometimes me living there. And maybe Mina. One day.

There was enough room at our house, too.

My room here is at the end of the hall. It's big but it doesn't have my bookshelf or my rug or my art supplies or my Unicorn Chronicles book posters on the walls. I don't like that it's bigger than my room at home; it just feels emptier. Like a hotel room where anyone could come and stay.

There's a window that overlooks the garden that Dad

and I are supposed to plant this summer. They had a seat built in special. Perfect for reading.

I set my duffel up there instead.

I roll my sleeping bag out next to the bed, which is made up with sheets that aren't my own.

The paint colors on the dresser are nice. I fan through the choices. *Inspired Lilac. Veri Berry. Spangle.* Naming paint colors must be the very best job. I hold the last one up to the wall and try to picture the whole room that color. It reminds me of the color of Starlight's horn. But I turn them over on the dresser, facedown.

I sit down on my sleeping bag and pull out my cell phone. I text Mom: "Miss you."

A second later, my phone chimes. "I miss you, too, Em," followed by a pink heart. I take a deep breath.

Pickle's followed me in here. Curled up by my feet, she looks like a lumpy pumpkin. I stroke her fur. Her whiskers twitch. She's no Bean, but she's not that bad, either. I don't hold the fact that she's Alice and Dad's cat against her. She's not the one who caused all this mess in the first place.

BOWLING NIGHT

It's crowded here," Dad says cheerfully, as we get out of the car at the far end of Ten Pin's parking lot. "I wonder if they're having some kind of event."

It's exactly like Dad not to check ahead of time. "What if we can't get a lane?" I ask.

Dad chuckles. "It'll be fine, Em. Don't worry."

I roll my eyes and hang back behind Dad and Alice, who are now holding hands in front of me. I pat one of Mina's old purses, which is hanging down by my hip. I've looped it across my body, but it somehow doesn't look as cool as it does on the girls in Hazel's magazine. In it, I've stuffed my paperback copy of *Nightshade and the Case of the Dastardly Dragon*. Emergency reading material.

The bowling alley is loud. We stand in line at the shoe counter. "Size?" the young guy asks me when we get to the front. He's wearing the official Ten Pin polo.

I step aside to let Dad and Alice in. "I'm not going to bowl," I say.

"Button." Dad puts his hand on my shoulder. "Be a sport."

"Size, Button?" The guy smirks. My face goes red, and I shrug off Dad's hand.

"Seven."

The guy sprays the shoes with sanitizer—a thick aerosol fog descending on top of them. I grab mine without saying thanks and head to our assigned lane ten. Lane ten is not the good lane. It's the lane where one of the bumpers from kiddie bowling permanently juts out. Broken.

There *is* an event tonight. Family leagues. I can't even believe it.

Dad logs our names into the scoring console. "B-U-T-T-O-N," he spells out loud, pretending to type it in, like what he said back at the shoe counter is funny.

"Just Em, Dad," I say. I slump down in the hard plastic chair.

There are all kinds of families here. Grandpas and grandmas with grandkids. Parents with teens as old as Mina. Moms and Dads with kids who actually need the bumpers up.

And us.

"Why don't you go test out a few of the balls?" Dad says.

I want to avoid him calling me Button in public again, so I agree. I walk over to the thin metal racks that sit just past the lanes. There's a purple sparkly one up top. I like the color and pick it up. Too heavy. I pick the pink marbled one next. It looks like a giant gumball.

I stick my fingers in the three holes to try it out.

"That one's too small," a familiar voice says next to me. "Your fingers will get jammed in there. You'll never get it down the lane."

It's Hector.

Have you ever been in a room where there's a constant noise? Like a buzzing light or the hum of an aquarium, but you don't actually hear it till someone points it out? Then you're super conscious of it? And it's always there?

Hector's exactly like that, I think. "Maybe try that green one," he says.

Until this year, I hadn't seen him anywhere. Suddenly he's everywhere.

First, the bookstore. Then the cafeteria and Ms. Arnold's room. And now Ten Pin Bowling Alley on a Friday night.

"Hey, Anita!" he calls out over the noise. He's so loud. "It's Emily. From school!"

"Em," I say, but he doesn't correct himself. "I like the pink." I hold on to it stubbornly.

Hector shrugs. He, and now Anita, who's jogged over

from their lane, are wearing matching bowling shirts with buttons down the front. Hector's is buttoned to the top and tucked into his shorts with a black belt. Anita's hangs loose over a navy blue strappy top. It looks kind of cool the way she wears it.

Hector pulls a red ball from the racks. He holds it up. It does kind of seem like he knows what he's doing.

"Are you here for the leagues?" Anita asks, looking over at Dad and Alice. Dad has his hand over hers and is guiding it in the bowling-ball-throwing motion. Like she needs any help. I turn away in disgust. "Are those your parents?"

"That's my dad." I pause. "And Alice, his . . . Alice, I guess."

"Huh," Anita says. "Looks like they like each other." *That's not the point*, I want to say. He's supposed to like Mom. But I keep my mouth shut.

"We're the Turkeys," Hector says, turning around to show me the back of his shirt. There's a giant appliqué turkey with its feathers shaped like colorful bowling pins.

"The Turkeys? Like Thanksgiving?"

"No, it's a bowling thing," Anita explains. "When you get three strikes in a row, it's a turkey." I nod like I understand. I've never been close to even getting one strike, so I guess I've never needed to know that.

"I wanted to be the Nightshades," Hector says. "But I was vetoed."

"It has nothing to do with bowling." Anita laughs.

"*Yet*," Hector says. "Maybe book ten will be *Nightshade and the Case of the Bowling Banshees*. It could happen." I don't say that I would have voted for the Nightshades, too.

An announcement comes over the loudspeaker signaling the start of the first game for the family bowlers. "We get a break between games two and three," Anita says. "If you're still here, meet us in the arcade, okay?"

"And use the green ball," Hector adds.

I nod, but when they leave, I stick with the pink.

"Were those your friends?" Dad asks when I return to our lane. Alice is perched on his knee like the teens in the food court. It's gross.

I shake my head. "Just kids from school."

"Well, you're up first," Alice says. The row on the screen with my name lights up. *EM*. At least Dad did that right.

I walk up, my bowling shoes smooth against the wood. I hold the ball out in front of me. Then I take a few steps, swinging my arm behind me first and then to the front. I release but my fingers stick. The ball thuds to the floor and rolls into the one bumperless gutter. Just my luck.

"You'll get it next time," Alice says encouragingly. Her cheerfulness only makes it worse.

"I got the wrong ball," I mumble. I grab the green one from the rack for my next turn.

I almost don't go to the arcade when I see some of the kids in the lanes next to us taking a break from their games. Maybe Anita will forget that she asked me to meet her. Or maybe she'll stay with her parents. But then I look at Alice and Dad, who are still sitting on top of each other like there aren't tons of empty seats around, and I think maybe I'll just go take a look.

Anita waves me over when she sees me. She's sitting at a little table in the café section with a huge plate of fries in front of her. "You have to eat some of these," she says.

I take one of them. They're smothered in orange cheese. "Where's Hector?"

She points to a pool table. There are two teen guys with pool cues and a bunch of the younger boys around the table watching. Hector stands a step or so back from the group. Even from here I can see there's leftover cheese on his mouth. Like a thick cheese lipstick. He laughs when the other boys laugh. He groans when the other boys groan. But somehow, even though he's with them, he's also not with them.

A tightness forms in my chest. I turn back to Anita.

"Are you and Hector twins?" I ask.

"Fraternal," she says. "He's the older one. By two minutes. Most people think he's my younger brother, though." She pauses. "He hates that."

"My sister's older, too. She's in high school."

"That's cool," Anita says. "She should come next time." I think about how heavy the bowling ball was in my hand. I wonder if Mina would even have the strength to hold it. "Hey, do you want to try the dance machine? It's open."

I follow her gaze. There's a giant glowing machine on a raised platform with handles you can hold on to and two grid-like footpads where you place your feet. "Okay," I say. We leave the fries, and Anita feeds two wrinkly dollars from her back pocket into the machine. We step onto the platform.

"Choose your dancer," an electronic voice commands. I pick a girl with funky blue hair and baggy jeans. Anita picks a girl that looks like her—brown skin, dark hair pulled up into a bun on the top of her head.

The machine starts counting down. My heart speeds up. "What am I supposed to do? What am I supposed to do?"

Anita points at the screen where two animated dancers stand. "Follow the arrows. Up, down, left, right. Sometimes you'll have to turn. Hang on to the handles for that." A nervous, excited feeling bubbles up in me. "Okay, here we go!"

The music starts. It's tricky at first. A left arrow here. A right arrow there. But then I get the hang of it and Anita and I are bouncing and laughing and turning in time to the music. By the time the song's over, there's a small crowd around us. "Totally Rad!" the game cheers as it tallies up our points.

Anita brushes a sweaty piece of hair from her face. "You've never done that before?"

I shake my head. "I took dance classes, so maybe that helped."

"Really? Me too! I take Jazz and Hip-Hop."

"I did mostly tap," I reply. "A little ballet."

I hear applause behind me. I turn around. It's Dad and Alice. They're smiling. Alice is holding my regular gym shoes and bag. "I guess it's time to go."

Anita leans over and gives me a quick hug. It surprises me. "See you on Monday."

We all return our shoes. I set mine on the counter real fast so the guy won't call me Button again. I'm relieved when he doesn't see me. Alice leans toward me. "Maybe you could invite that girl over. She seemed nice."

"Anita? I dunno. She's just my locker buddy," I say. "Maybe I'll invite Hazel."

Out of the corner of my eye I see that Hector's rejoined Anita at the table. They're laughing together, and he waves the cheesiest fry in my direction. I look away.

It's a warm night. In the car on the way back to Dad's, he rolls the windows down and taps on the steering wheel in time to the music—some nineties song I don't recognize. Alice sings along like she's a regular backup singer. When there's a pause, he says, "Wasn't that great? Maybe we should join the family league," like it's the best idea ever.

All the good feelings I had built up whoosh out of me like air from a flattened bike tire. "It's for *families*, Dad."

Even over the music I can hear Dad take in a breath to say something. Alice puts her hand on his. She shakes her head.

MOVEMENT!

We start each Language Arts class with silent reading time. Ms. Arnold reads, too. That Monday, she's lounged back in her chair and her feet are propped up on her desk. She's wearing these bell-bottom-like pants and brown clogs, which probably shouldn't look cool but do. I sneak glances at her book—Anastasia something. The last name starts with a *K* but I can't read it from where I'm sitting.

I sneak a peek at Hector's book, too, while I'm stretching out my back from sleeping on the floor all weekend. It's a graphic novel with picture panels of robots zapping each other with lasers. I can hear the pages crinkle as he turns them; it must be brand new.

Ms. Arnold glances up and I meet eyes with her. She smiles. When reading time is almost through, she walks over to my desk. She kneels down next to me and leans in so only I can hear her. "You know, Emily, if you ever want to read something different—and I'm not saying you do—but I think these might be a good choice." She hands me the book she was reading. The *K* word is Krupnik. *Anastasia Krupnik*. There's a girl on the front—must be Anastasia—with big glasses surrounded by a bunch of papers. "I know it looks a little old-fashioned, but I love these books."

"I'll think about it," I say. I make a show of opening the Unicorn Chronicles book four back up and looking very intently at the page. I'm not sure why I'd want to read anything different when I love these characters and stories so much.

"Okay," she says. She pats my shoulder. Then she goes back up to the front of the room and claps her hands together. Reading time is over. "Let's talk about informational writing!" She writes it on the board, complete with an exclamation point. A couple of people in the class groan; she ignores them. "Today, we're going to start our first writing project for the year. It's going to be a partner project."

Kids are already making eye contact with each other across the room and nodding. They're pairing up; no one's looking at me. I rub my hands on my shorts. "Not so fast,"

Ms. Arnold says. "I've randomly put you in pairings, which you'll get in a moment. It's important to get to know how to work with different kinds of people."

She hands a stack of papers to the front of each row. Hector passes me one over his shoulder. The heading at the top of it says "MOVEMENT!"

"You and your partner will choose a nonfiction topic related to movement. Maybe you want to research the transcontinental railroad. Or maybe you want to write a report on Rosa Parks, whose deliberate lack of movement on a bus helped push a nation forward during the civil rights era. Or maybe you'll connect it to your current science studies about migration. Once you have your topic, you'll research together and craft some kind of informative presentation— whether it's written or oral—that educates your classmates about your topic."

"You'll have class time," she continues. "But you'll also need to work together outside school—in person or online."

She picks up a clipboard off her desk and starts reading the pairings. "Clare Pavell and Ronald Atwater. Tricia Hannah and Jenna Mar. Hector Garcia and Em Murphy."

I watch as Hector writes my name in the partner spot on his paper. I leave mine blank. The second Ms. Arnold finishes reading the list, I pop out of my seat and run up to her desk. I think about Friday night at the bowling alley. His cheese-crusted grin. His tucked-in shirt. The way he doesn't seem to fit in. I'm starting to feel a little bit desperate. I just can't be paired up with him.

"I think there's been a mistake," I whisper. I look up. Hector's watching me. "I can't work with Hector." I'm picturing Lucy starting to call me Soap Girl and sneaking a bar of soap into *my* desk. I try to sniff myself without being too obvious about it, as if somehow Hector's not-bad-at-all smell could have rubbed off on me.

"Has he been mean to you?" she asks, concerned. I shake my head. "Do you feel like he won't do his share of work?"

"No," I say in a small voice. "I think he will do the work."

"Is there any good reason you can't work together?" I'm quiet.

Ms. Arnold purses her lips. "To be honest, I didn't expect this from you." My hands grow tingly and I shove them into my pockets. I think about how rotten the words coming out of my mouth probably sounded. "Hector will be an excellent partner to work with."

"Okay, yeah." I can't even look at her now. I just stare red-faced at the floor. I feel so wrong-side-out these days. I slink back to my seat and slide into it.

Hector turns around. "So what are you thinking?" He doesn't ask why I was just up at Ms. Arnold's desk or why there's a blank next to "partner name" on my sheet. "It might be cool to do space travel or, like, what about the movement of people? Ooh, what about the gold rush?"

I jot them down in the idea box on my paper. My normally smooth handwriting is shaky.

"We should get together soon to start," he says. "You could come over to my house."

"I might not have a ride," I say. "You could come over to mine, I guess."

"Sure!" Hector says. "My dad can bring me. I'll bring over the new Unicorn Chronicles/Robots of Doom super special."

"Really?!" I say, forgetting that I'm not supposed to be excited about any of this with Hector. "What do you think of them doing this? I mean, robots and unicorns?"

"It's awesome," Hector says. His eyes get this sparkliness to them. "Think about all the new story lines and all the characters. There could be a thousand more books. Besides—can you imagine Nightshade and Robotical pairing up on a mystery?" He makes a motion like fireworks are coming out of his head. "Mind blown."

When I get home that afternoon, the telephone is ringing. I drop my backpack in the hall and grab it on the third ring, smooshing the receiver next to my ear. "Hello?"

"Hey, Emily." It's Mina. She's upbeat. Today must be a good day. Even so, I'm anxious.

"Hi," I say in a quiet voice. I wish I hadn't picked up. On Wednesdays, there's at least Evie and Mom in the room. I can be as quiet as I want sitting on my corner of the couch. I don't want to say the wrong thing. The phone is harder. "Mom's not home."

"I know," she says. "I called to talk to you. How's school?" I picture Mina curled up on the wooden bench in the phone booth. There are two of them, right off Pinehurst's main room. They're not allowed to have their own cell phones.

There's a loud knocking in the background. A muffled voice. It startles me. "It's loud there."

"Yeah, hold on." I picture Mina cupping her hand over the receiver. "I just got in here," she yells. Then, "Sorry." Her voice is clear now. "So tell me about things. Is your locker in the blue hallway? Is Mr. Georges still there?"

"Mr. Georges?"

"Lunchroom monitor," she says. "Always something on his tie."

I think back to the first day of school and the man with the mustard-stained tie in the cafeteria and all that went with it. "Yeah, I think so."

"Did you make new friends? How's Hazel?"

Mina can't see the knot that's formed in my stomach. Maybe telling her would start to unravel it. But then I think about how big Mina's problems are and how small and unimportant mine are in comparison. "She's fine."

"Oh," she says. She almost sounds disappointed. "Are you going to do any clubs? I did newspaper. Remember that? And choir! What about choir?"

"Maybe."

Mina takes a deep breath. "Emily. I just want to talk to you." She's starting to sound frustrated. "I want to hear about school."

"I know," I say. I twist the phone cord around my finger again and again until the tip of it turns red. "I want to talk to you, too. But I've got to let Bean out and I have all this homework. . . ."

"Fine. You can have the phone now," she says to the girl probably still waiting outside the glass door. She doesn't bother covering up her end of the telephone this time. "I'll talk to you later. Okay?" She doesn't wait for an answer. She hangs up the phone.

My hand shakes as I put the phone back in its cradle.

Just a year ago, we had set up a telephone system between our rooms. Plastic Solo cups attached with string. It had been for my fifth-grade Science Spectacular project, and we had come up with different trials to see which one worked best. Mina and I tested four types: yarn, a thick thread, fishing line, and the kind of thin metal you curl into jewelry. We could hear each other so clearly with the fishing line that we left it up for weeks, even after we had taken pictures of it for my tri-fold board. We'd talk to each other, late into the night, through closed doors. We had so much to say.

Up in my room, I flop down on my bed and groan. Bean leaps up to join me and licks my face. She always knows what to do. I roll over and grab my laptop. I flip it open and click on my email. There's one from the Unicorn Chronicles fan forum site.

From: Unicorn Underworld Fan Forums
To: Emily Murphy (UnicornGirl11)
Date: August 29 at 3:45 a.m.
Subject: MOVIE COUNTDOWN

Hey Chroniclers!
Whether you are Team Nightshade, Team Starlight, or Team Disastero (ha! Yeah right!), we bet you are getting pumped up for the brand new Unicorn Chronicles movie. We cannot wait to see our favorite characters in action again on the big screen. We know that not everyone will be able to see the movie on the very first day, SO we are going to set up a special thread on the forums just for you early moviegoers to discuss all the spoilers you want!

As always, feel free to send us your fan art, fan fiction, or fan pics. You could be our featured fan of the day.

Thirty-two days! Ahh!

—The Unicorn Chronicles Fan Forum Team

I squeal out loud. Only thirty-two days! I can't believe it's so soon. I draw an extra yellow star on my calendar. I still need to talk about the plans for the movie with Hazel. I make a point not to look at Mina's coming-home date.

I pull my planner out of my backpack. I scroll down my assignments. I should get started on my math homework, but I keep glancing over to my CD player and notes sitting on the edge of my desk.

I pop in the second CD, prop some pillows against my headboard, and join Bean on my bed. I press play. The music starts.

"Hello again. I'm Dr. Franklinton-Morehouse. I'm so glad you're continuing on this journey to be the best YOU possible along with us. Let's review. Last session, you explored who you currently are. You left room in your chart for who you'll be at the end of our sessions."

Before Emily and After Emily. I put a star on my paper next to the After.

"What I need you to do now is get moving in the right

direction. But we need to know what this new and better you looks like. You need a goal. I'd like you to take a moment now and write down a definition—just like in the dictionary. Define who this new YOU would be."

The music starts up again.

I take a clean sheet of notebook paper from the pile. I write my name in my best, curliest cursive:

Em Murphy (noun).
Cool.
Girl who fits in.
Best friends with Hazel.
Friends with Lucy, Annemarie, and Gina.
Knows the right things to do (hair, boy stuff, clothes).
Fancy-pants.

"Good," Dr. Franklinton-Morehouse says. "This is what you'll come back to. I'd like you to hang it up where you can see it. A constant reminder. In spare moments of your day, I want you to visualize this person. How do they talk? How do they act? Try it now. When this CD ends, I want you to imagine the person you've just described."

The CD whirs to a stop.

Bean nuzzles up to me. I love her sweet doggy breath. I give her a kiss on the nose. "Okay, Bean, I need to visualize. Perfect me, perfect me."

I close my eyes. I picture a girl. There are other girls around her. They're laughing at her jokes. Her hair is swishy and super straight and shiny, almost like it's full of sunshine itself. She's wearing skinny black pants and Converse sneakers and her shirt is straight out of the newest *Teen Scene*. Her lips are the most perfect shade of pink because she's wearing this secret lip gloss that's probably made of magic or crystals or something.

Everyone wants to sit with her at lunch. In fact, people get up just to make room.

Perfect me has no problems. Her mom and dad are together, still living in their small house on Persimmon Way. They go on road trips. To Florida, I think. Family vacations to the brand new Unicorn Chronicles Magical Underworld theme park. Perfect me knows how to talk to her sister on the phone. She knows how to say the right things to make everything okay.

I sigh.

It's the exact opposite of who I am now.

BE THE BALLOON

Tuesday morning before school, we're in the dining room having breakfast. It's so early it's still dark out and Bean is snoozing away on her folded-up blanket in the corner of the room. There's a new painting on the wall. Well, not new, but one Mom dug up from the basement To Keep pile. She shined up the frame last night with cleaning polish, and we hung it up together while Bean supervised.

It looks nice, like it's always belonged up there.

Mom has her reading glasses on and her coffee, but it's still pretty much filled to the top. I'm sure it's cold now. Puzzle Time magic. She's scanning the pieces looking for one with a little squiggle of yellow. We almost have South America completed.

"Oh, there it is," I say, pointing to a piece on the very edge of the table with my spoon.

"Good eye," she says and fits the piece into place. She takes her glasses off, sets them on the table, and leans back in her chair. It's a bad sign. It's a sign of a Big Conversation.

"So," Mom says. "When Mina comes home, Dad and Alice are going to come over for dinner." It comes out in a rush, like she's ripping off a Band-Aid. She waits a second, maybe staring at my open mouth or the way my face is becoming red around the cheeks. "All of us together." As if I needed the clarification.

"Mom. No." Take one uncomfortable thing, Mina coming home, and smoosh it together with another uncomfortable thing, Dad and Alice coming over. It's a recipe for disaster. "Dad doesn't even come to Mina's stuff on Wednesdays!"

Mom sighs. She rubs her forehead in her hands. "I know. It's hard for him."

"It's hard for him? He's a grown-up!" I'm exasperated now. A little bit of me is afraid I'm going to upend this puzzle if I'm not careful. "This is hard for me, too!"

Mom takes both of my hands in hers. "I know. I know. Your dad is a grown-up. And grown-ups sometimes have to face hard things. But it doesn't make it less difficult. Or someone more ready."

"But you're facing it."

"I am. But I don't have a choice. She's my daughter."

She's Dad's daughter, too. But Dad, he can escape all this in his big block house with Alice. Out of sight, out of mind, while Mom and I are trapped here.

I never asked for this.

"I still don't want them to come." I pull my hands away and cross my arms over my chest. My eyes prickle and I can feel the tears building behind them. Bean raises her left eyebrow at me. Her tail beats once against the ground in solidarity. It's nice to have someone on my side, even if she's a dog.

"Evie feels like it could be a good first step. And Dad's willing, so . . ." Of course Evie would say that. She's not the one living here. My body tenses from my shoulders down to my stomach. "It's a lot for Dad to come. I know that's hard for you to understand."

I feel like we're right on the edge of something. Of Mom telling me a real truth—that sometimes people don't act the way we think they should. That sometimes Dad doesn't act like a dad at all. But I want to hear her say it. "Then explain it!"

Mom closes up. She gives me a sad smile. "We have to do what's best for Mina."

What about what's best for me? I want to ask.

Instead I say, "Okay. Okay," even though it's not. I go upstairs to get ready for school.

When I get to school, I'm glad to see that the hallways are empty. It gives me the room I feel I need to breathe. I lean my head back against the cool metal of the locker.

Then, cutting through the quiet of the morning, there's a sound. A cheer.

I'm curious, so I start walking in the direction of the sound and end up right in front of Ms. Arnold's door. It's open but there's this homemade sign on it that says *Bagel Bunch* with a dancing bagel. I know Sara drew it; I can tell.

Maybe this is the club Ms. Arnold told me about. I guess it has a name now.

The sign's definitely not written in her neat teacher handwriting, and it's affixed with a piece of bright green tape. I peek around the door. Ms. Arnold's sitting in one of the student desks and she's taking a bite of a giant bagel. Blueberry, I think. In her other hand are four playing cards.

I lean a little closer so I can get a better look. There's Anita and Hector and Lloyd and Sara. They're smiling. Laughing. I watch as Sara nudges Anita on the shoulder and gives her a knowing glance. A friend glance. A me-and-Hazel glance.

It fills me with this sudden sadness and longing I didn't know were there.

But before I can think on it, they lunge forward to the center of the circle and startle me out of my thoughts.

"Whoo-hoo!" I hear. "Yes!"

Suddenly, Hector's up and dancing around the circle with a marker in his hand. Then he looks straight at me watching them from the door. "Hey! Hey, guys! It's Em Murphy."

"Emily," Ms. Arnold says. She stands, not even caring that there're crumbs all over her pants. I bet Dr. Franklinton-Morehouse would say she's comfortable with who she is. Her smile turns to concern when she sees my red eyes and cheeks that have stayed blotchy. "Is everything all right? Why don't you join us?"

"Yes, Emily," Hector says. He's walking around with his arms out like he's a zombie. "Join us. We've come to eat your brains."

Anita swats him on the arm. "Hector!" she says and walks to the door. She grabs my hand and squeezes. It's nice. Reassuring, like it's squeezing some of the sadness away through sheer force. "He means bagels. They're really good. We play cards, too, but it didn't all fit on the sign."

"I could draw the bagel with cards in his hand," Sara suggests.

Hector raises his marker. "Yes, brilliant. You should do

that with my winning marker. We ran out of spoons," he says, as if that will make any sense to me.

"It's our first meeting," Lloyd says. "We're BREAKFAST ENTHUSIASTS." He says it like he's some kind of super-hero and thrusts his bagel high in the air. His sleeve dangles off his arm. They're always huge. Hand-me-down shirts, I guess. Mina's in the same grade as one of his brothers, and I know he has a few more.

There's cream cheese on the cuffs of them now, but no one seems to be paying any attention to that. Hector bumps Lloyd's bagel with his own. "Breakfast!"

"Breakfast!" they cheer together.

"There won't be bagels every week," Ms. Arnold says. "Just today."

"But maybe every Tuesday." Lloyd says this with his mouth practically full, so it comes out a little garbled.

Ms. Arnold laughs and pats him on the shoulder. "We'll see what we can do. Teacher budget, remember?"

"Um, thanks," I say, backing up slowly from the door.

"You should join," Sara says. She finishes up drawing the cards in the bagel's hand. She smiles her shy smile. I look at the rest of them—Anita resetting the cards, Hector now in a deep conversation with Lloyd about zombies and brains and Bigfoot maybe (from the words I can hear), and Sara who holds the marker still.

But I picture the T chart in my notebook. I'm not sure that member of the Bagel Bunch is part of the After.

I shake my head.

I turn to leave, when Ms. Arnold catches me by the shoulder. "Really, Emily. Are you sure you're okay? I'm worried about you."

I swallow hard. "Yeah. I'm fine."

Hector yells something about our project as I walk out the door. Something about the movement of zombies.

All day long, I try to think about other things besides Mina coming home and all of us together for dinner. But problems are like sunburns, I think. You can forget about it for a little while, but an unfortunate shift of a T-shirt and suddenly you're in pain again. It's always there.

After school, I just want to see my best friend. Not at our lunch table, where Lucy's always a step away. Not in the hallway that's crowded and loud. Just me and her alone. Hazel's house isn't too far, but I grab the CD player from my desk anyway. I need to hear what Dr. Franklinton-Morehouse has to say. Maybe he has some guidance for me.

"Greetings," he says. "I am so glad to be able to continue with you on this journey to self-discovery and being the best you that you can be. Today I want to talk to you about some actionable steps you can take. The first: you must be willing to change."

He chuckles. "Now, I know what you're thinking. You're thinking you've bought the CDs, of course you're willing to change. But consider this. What if a person makes it a goal to eat more vegetables? They go to the grocery. They purchase carrots and eggplants and celery and lettuce. Then they let them sit in their refrigerator, uneaten. See, the intention was there, but the follow-up was not. Intention and follow-up. Peanut butter and jelly. You must have both."

"So here is my challenge: you must do something you don't want to do. Picture your life as a balloon. Think about what people do before they blow one up. That's right! They stretch it. This, in turn, allows more air to be let in; for the shape of the balloon to grow bigger than they thought possible."

"Stretch yourself today," he says. "Be the balloon."

Hazel is lying on her bed, her arms down by her sides, her hair fanned out around her head like a mermaid. Her eyes are closed.

Big Norm the gerbil *scritch-scritches* in his glass case—oblivious to it all. He's making a giant pile of cedar shavings in the corner. A castle. He's king of his own tiny animal kingdom. He doesn't have to worry about a thing. I give him a little carrot piece from his treat dish next to the case. I love how he holds it in his little hands.

"What are you doing?" I ask, flopping down on Hazel's

giant beanbag chair. It's perfectly molded to my shape from all the times I've sat there.

"Shh...," she says. Her eyes stay closed. "I'm visualizing."

I think about the CDs. "I'm visualizing, too. Not right now, but earlier. What are you visualizing?"

"The game tomorrow. Coach says we should visualize success. Each play, each move. It should be like a movie in our mind." She pops up at this, her face red from the sudden movement. "Pro athletes do this. Like the bobsled. The team will visualize the course. What about you?"

I open my mouth to tell her about the CDs, but I hesitate. I'm not sure why. Normally it's so easy to tell Hazel everything. I clear my throat and try something else. "Mina's coming home this week."

"What?!" Hazel's suddenly animated. "Em, oh my gosh. Why didn't you tell me? Like, you should have come in this room and been like, 'MINA'S COMING HOME THIS WEEK!! Ahh!'" She kicks her feet a little against the bed. "Are you so excited?"

"Yeah, but . . ." My stomach somersaults.

"But what?"

I shrug, the words stuck inside me.

"When do you think I can come see her? Soon, right?"

My hands start to sweat, so I just nod and change the subject. "Did you get that email from the forum?" Hazel joined the same time I did. She's StarlightHaze. I think it's pretty clever. More clever than UnicornGirl11. "Only thirty-one days till the movie!"

"I haven't been on," Hazel says. "I get home so late and then I have to eat dinner and then homework. You know . . ." She lets her voice trail off.

But I kind of don't know at all.

"We're still going together, though, right?"

Hazel stands and leans over Big Norm's glass home. She brushes the sign we made for him with her hip. *Big Norm* is written in these sticker letters we got from the craft store. We drew him, too; he looks like a giant Oreo cookie with his black-and-white coloring. We even gave him heart eyes.

The edges of the paper are worn and the tape is yellowed but it's still there.

"Yeah, about that—" Hazel starts.

"What?" I say. "Don't you want to go anymore?" I swallow hard.

"I do," Hazel says. "But Annemarie's having her birthday party, and she's doing a movie. I think we'll be seeing the Unicorn Chronicles one."

I blink rapidly and look at anything but Hazel. It's then that I notice the poster on her wall, next to her dresser. It says *Field Hockey Players Kick Grass* in these white block letters with two field hockey sticks positioned together like hearts.

"Where'd your Nightshade poster go?" She used to have one in that very same spot with Nightshade and Starlight holding up their magnifying glasses to their eyeballs like they could see right through you. A team.

Hazel shrugs. "In my closet." My stomach clenches. "I think. Anyways, you're invited. It just won't be me and you, though. That's okay, right?"

I can't stop staring at the new poster. "I didn't get an invitation." I cross my arms over my chest and know that everything's coming out in a huff. This isn't how I expected this to go at all.

"You just did. I'm telling you now," she says sharply. "It's not like last year when you'd get a card in the mail or something. People just ask." I wonder when Hazel's learned so much about everything. "And besides . . ." She comes over and shakes my shoulder in this good-natured kind of way. Her words are softer now. "They're our friends."

Your friends, I want to say.

There was this game we'd play in first grade on the playground called Circle Break. It's a dumb name, but also self-explanatory, and we were in first grade so everything was kind of obvious. Everyone would stand in a circle with their hands held tight. One person would try to run at the group and break through the arms into the center.

I was never very good at it.

But I think about Dr. Franklinton-Morehouse's words I heard on the way over. About trying things that are uncomfortable. Maybe he's talking about dinner with Dad and Alice. Maybe he's talking about the movie.

But what if that balloon stretches too far?

Still, I need to try.

"Yeah," I say, knowing I need to do it. I try not to think about all the other years when it's just been me and Hazel, or me and Mina and Hazel. "That'll be great."

WELCOME HOME, MINA

On the day Mina comes home, I spend half the afternoon in the nurse's office because my stomach hurts so bad, and I feel light-headed and weak. He offers to call Mom and then Dad, but I don't really want to see either of them right now, so I tell her they're busy. I want a few final moments just to myself in the good quiet, and if that has to be while lying on the green cot under a disposable blanket in the clinic, that's fine.

When the bus drops me off on my street, I take an extra-long time walking from the main road to the house. Dad's car is already in the driveway. I wonder if maybe I should just keep walking. I could. People do that. I read about a guy who walked from California to New York with just his dog.

It's tempting. I could just grab Bean and go. Instead, I grab the mail out of the box and let myself in through the garage door.

Dad and Alice are in the kitchen. Alice is chopping a red pepper into thin slices and Dad is slicing chicken and looking at a recipe card that Mom must have left behind for him. Bean's in the kitchen, too, sprawled out on the hardwood floor next to Alice's feet. She doesn't even get up. Traitor. I frown, even though I don't entirely mean it.

Dad wipes his hands on Mom's apron that he's tied around his waist. He's wearing a blue-and-white checkered shirt. That, combined with the beard he started to grow when he first moved out, makes him look like a lumberjack. A lumberjack in the middle of Ohio.

Ridiculous.

Mom calls it his midlife crisis. Not to me, though. To Aunt Bea on the phone.

"How'd you get in?" I ask, dropping my book bag next to the kitchen table.

"Button! Hello to you, too," Dad says, as if all this—him and Alice cooking in *our* kitchen—is totally normal. "And the hide-a-key in the rock next to the front porch." I make a mental note to change its location. If this isn't Dad's house anymore, he doesn't need to know where the key is. I slip onto the stool at the counter.

"What are you making?" I ask.

"Chicken with sautéed vegetables and potatoes." Alice is opening and closing the cabinets looking for something. I let her look for a minute. Finally she says, "Pot?"

"Bottom cabinet on the left," I say.

"Ah," she says, and pulls out what she's looking for. "Got it!" She fills it with water from the sink.

Dad opens his mouth. I expect him to ask something about Mina. I dread him asking something about Mina. "So tell me about school," Dad says instead. "How's that going?"

I'm angry and relieved all at once. "Fine."

"Fine and . . ." He looks at me expectantly.

I sigh. "Uh—we're starting these projects. With partners. About movement."

"Very cool, Button. With Hazel?" he asks because I've always done my projects with her.

"With Hector." Dad looks at me. "That kid from the bowling alley. In the turkey shirt."

"Ahh, yes." He doesn't ask me how I feel about it. "You know, if you need an expert, movement is my specialty." He starts shaking his hips and doing these dumb moves that I bet he thinks will make me laugh. Then he starts to whistle this happy tune. Like life in general is easy and breezy.

I can't stand it.

"I made decorations," I announce. "To welcome Mina home. I'm going to go get them."

"That's really nice, Em," Alice says. She's peeling a large potato over the trash can now. "I'd be happy to help you put them up. If you need help, that is."

"I'm good." The sound of Dad's whistling follows me upstairs.

Up in my room, I pull out the decorations that I made back when I first thought Mina was going to come home. A few are crumpled, but I smooth them flat. They still look pretty good. There are music notes decorated with black glitter and letters that spell *Hi Mina!* punched out from my letter set. I didn't have the right ones for *Welcome Home*. There are also some random hearts and stars and a rainbow because those things are cheerful and welcoming and say, "I'm happy you're here." Even if I'm not so certain about that myself.

I grab the tape out of my drawer and bring everything downstairs.

Alice is laying out one of Mom's nice tablecloths on our kitchen table. We'd fit better around the dining room table, but that's not an option anymore.

"Where'd Dad go?" I ask.

"I'm in here," he answers from the dining room.

I stick a loop of tape on the back of a music note and go find him. Dad's leaning over the puzzle Mom and I've been working on. He's putting France into place.

I go up behind him and take the piece out and put it back into the pile. "Me and Mom have got this," I snap. "We've been working on it *together*."

He turns around and looks at me sadly. "I'm sorry, Button. It looks good." For a moment, my chest tenses up, but I shrug out from his touch.

"Mina will be here soon." I let Dad walk out first. I roll the door closed behind us.

A few minutes later, I hear Mina and Mom come through the front door.

Whenever friends or Aunt Bea or the refrigerator repair person comes over, they go through the front door. Mom insists on it. Something about not seeing all the junk and dust collecting in the garage, but Mina's not supposed to be a guest.

"We're here," Mom says, even though we know. We heard the latch of the door and the creak as it opened. It's hard to sneak around anywhere in this house. I watch Mina from my place at the counter. I don't move. I hold my breath.

Mina looks better—her cheeks are flushed pink and her clothes don't droop off her like they used to. Her shoulders are softer and less sharp.

I know enough from reading the brochures that I'm not supposed to talk about how she looks. But they didn't necessarily tell me what I *should* say, either.

Bean trots into the hallway. She eyes Mina carefully and sniffs her left sneaker, then the right one. She takes deep whiffs of Mina's pant leg.

"She doesn't remember me," Mina says dully.

Mom sets down Mina's suitcase on the rug and smooths Mina's sleeve. "Of course she does, honey." Mina doesn't look convinced.

Dad sets down the knife, and he and Alice step into the hallway. Alice hangs back, wringing the dish towel in her hands, and Dad steps forward, arms outstretched, to hug Mina. His arms move stiffly like he's rusty at this.

He catches Mina's shoulder.

A feeling like all this has happened before washes over me.

THEN AND NOW

It was late June.

I had just come home from a sleepover at Hazel's. Mina was at work, so I expected there to be breakfast sounds coming out of the kitchen: bacon sizzles and the little hiss butter makes when it's dropped on the griddle. When Mina was gone, it was okay to make good breakfast.

But instead it was too quiet. There was something wrong.

I heard Mom's voice. "Mina, open the door."

My first thought was slight disappointment that Mina wasn't at work. My second thought was that it was strange to hear Mom asking. The week before, she had taken the screwdriver from Dad's old tool kit he left behind in the garage and removed Mina's doorknob so she couldn't lock her door anymore.

Mina liked to be closed up where no one could see her or her secret exercising or her secret notebook. But her secrets had crept out. They hung in our house like cobwebs in the corners. "I'm going to count to three"—Mom used her firm voice—"and then I'm coming in."

"Leave me alone," Mina screamed. I winced.

Sometimes it was better if I tiptoed into my room and was super quiet so no one had to worry about me. Other times, it was better if I went to comfort Mina. I'd run my hands through her hair like we used to when we played salon when we were little. I tried not to think about how thin it had gotten.

I was wondering what to do next when Dad stepped into the hallway. "Button," he said and held out his hand.

Dad. He looked so strange leaning against the door frame. "What are you doing here?" I said. He was supposed to be with Alice in their brand-new house.

"Button," he said again, like I hadn't even asked him a question. He lumbered toward me with these slow, careful steps, and I realized that he was there because something terrible must have happened.

"Is it Grandma Bebe?" But how could it be Grandma

Bebe? She had sent a postcard just last week from her home in Boca Raton. There were palm trees and blue water and sand and curvy cursive words that read *Wish You Were Here*. And I did. I wanted to be anywhere but our house.

"No, no, she's fine." Dad laid his heavy hand on my shoulder. "Listen." He half knelt down so we were at eye level. "Mina's going to go away."

That didn't make any kind of sense. I guess my mind was still on the postcard, so I said, "To visit Grandma?"

"No, Emily. To get better. Mina's sick."

"I thought we were helping her here," I said. I think of all the doctor's visits and dinners and Mom crying and Mina crying and me crying.

Mina burst out of her room. The door hit against the wall with the force of it. "Emily," Mina shouted when she turned and saw me at the bottom of the stairs. "Emily!" I saw Bean's head peek around the corner of the hallway railing. "They're sending me away." She heaved a piece of paper down the stairs.

I picked it up. It was a brochure. The cover was smooth and shiny. There was a picture of girls walking along a gravel path lined with grass and flowers.

PINEHURST: A Residential Treatment Facility. A place for girls like Mina.

"Mina, please." Mom's voice is quiet now. "You need

more help than we can give you here at home." The brochure fell limp against my side.

"You've given up on me!" Mina yelled. Her shoulders shook with giant silent sobs. I could see the sharpness of her bones through her T-shirt.

"No, no. Never," Mom said, reaching a hand out to Mina.

But Mina crossed her arms over her chest. I couldn't look at her red and splotchy, too-sharp face. "I hate you all," she said.

I stood, still as a statue. It felt like she was talking right to me.

I'm a statue now again. Two months later.

I should say something. "I made you decorations."

Mina shifts in her sneakers like it's uncomfortable to stand there, even though it's been only a few minutes.

After a moment, she says, "Thanks." Her voice is flat.

I try to smile. I attempt to pull my face tight. But I can't. Even though Mina looks different, things don't feel different. Nothing has changed at all.

"FAMILY" DINNER

've got to give Alice credit for trying. She's bought Mina's favorite flowers and arranged them in one of Grandma's old vases in the middle of the table. I'm glad because it eclipses Mina a little bit, like Earth moving in front of the moon. If I move my head to the left, I can pretend she's not there.

I can't say the same for Dad.

"I was thinking," he says, chewing thoughtfully on a piece of chicken, "that we could do three raised beds this summer. Carrots, lettuce, and peppers. Maybe a salsa garden. Some tomatoes?"

"I didn't know you were so into gardening, Adam." Mom's voice is pinched. She stabs a piece of squash with her fork and smiles up at him, but the smile doesn't reach her eyes. I see her sneaking glances at Mina, who is staring at her plate.

"I've always been into agriculture, Maura," he says. He turns to me next. "So what do you think?

"About agriculture?" I don't feel I've really formed any firm opinions on the topic, so I stay quiet. I keep sneaking glances at Mina, too. I try to make it look like I'm admiring the flowers when really I'm watching Mina's jaw go tight.

In an instant, she pushes away the plate. "I don't want this." Bean runs from her place under my chair into the family room.

"Mina, please," Mom says. Her face looks pained. "These are some of your favorite foods." She puts her hand over Mina's.

My throat closes. I take a huge gulp of water like it might somehow help and blurt out the first thing that comes to mind. "Sorry about the sign. I wanted to write out *Welcome Home Mina*." I'm nervous talking now. "But I didn't have enough letters." The *i* in *Mina* has fallen to the floor, though, so now it says *Hi Mna*, like we're welcoming some entirely different girl into our house.

Mina doesn't even look at it. She just stares at her plate. I used all that glitter for nothing.

"My stomach hurts."

"Evie said that could happen," Mom explains. "It's normal." She's pleading now.

Mina ignores her. She gestures at Dad and Alice with her fork. "I don't want them to be here." I kind of wish she had gestured at me, too, because right now I don't want to be here. A little part of me doesn't want Mina to be here, either. Alice looks down at her hands.

"Don't do this," Dad says. I can see a little bit of red creeping up his neck. It's the closest I've seen him get to angry in a long while. Maybe it's hard to pretend everything's okay when it's right in your face.

"Don't do what?" Mina asks. The way she stares at him, it's as if her eyeballs have developed lasers. "I'm sorry if this isn't what you expected. Not everything can be happy all the time." Her words sting even me.

Dad opens his mouth, then closes it. Finally, he says, "I just want to have a nice dinner. All of us together." He looks so lost, like he doesn't have the right words anymore. Maybe that's why he didn't come on Wednesdays. He didn't know what to say.

I didn't know what to say either, but I still came.

"You never cared about seeing me when I was at Pinehurst." Her voice is thick now and her eyes start to well. "Why didn't you come?"

Dad holds his hands flat, palms out in front of him. "I

had to work," he tries. His shoulders lift. "I don't know."

Mina shakes her head. "Can I eat this later, please? I just want to go to my room."

Dad pushes away from the table. "Maybe it's best if we go." He sounds tired. Relieved maybe. "We can try again next week." He puts his hand on Mina's shoulder. She turns away.

Alice stands, too. Mom walks them to the door, leaving me and Mina, half-eaten dinner plates, and this uncomfortable, heavy feeling in the air.

I clear my throat. "Um, I'm glad you're home." It seems like the right thing to say.

Mina just puts her head on the table. "This sucks," she says. She gives a big shuddery sigh. It's like she doesn't even hear me.

Later that night, I creep downstairs because my stomach is growling. I barely got to eat myself. I don't want the leftovers from that evening's dinner, but I'll take anything else. When I get to the bottom of the stairs, I freeze. There's a light on in the kitchen. It's the one over the sink and not very bright, so it makes everything look lonely and sad. Mina and Mom are at the kitchen table. Mina has one of her special milk shakes in a can in front of her. She told me about those. The girls had to drink them after their dinners. She hates them.

I can see Mina's shoulders shaking.

"Come on, Mina," Mom says. Her voice is soft. "You're almost done." Mina pinches her nose shut and drains the rest of the glass. She cries. Mom reaches out and rubs her shoulder. I sneak away, quiet.

I lie in my bed awake that night for a long time.

WEEKEND BREAKFAST

When Mina's home, food is the sun and we all revolve around it.

When Mina was away, I'd grab a Pop-Tart and eat it in Mom's car on the way to the Y's summer day camp or the neighborhood pool. Breakfast wasn't something I thought about. It's just something I did. Now there are place mats on the table and Mom's standing in front of the stove in her bare-stocking feet making scrambled eggs and toast with jam and butter. There's bacon in the oven. I can smell it.

It's special weekend breakfast on a regular weekday.

Mina can smell it, too, I think, because her footsteps are slow on the steps, like she's taking her good old time coming downstairs on purpose. When she finally gets into the kitchen she sets her book bag down on the table. I sneak little glances at her. She riffles through her papers in super-slow motion, even though I can't even imagine what she's looking for because she hasn't gone to actual high school this fall.

Mom just waits and doesn't say a word.

Finally, Mina wrinkles her nose. "What is all this?"

"Breakfast."

"I'm not hungry, though. My stomach hurts." She wraps her arms around her waist in emphasis.

"Mina." Mom's voice is level. "You need to eat the breakfast I'm making you because it's on your meal plan. Our job is to follow the meal plan."

"But how did you make it?" She looks anxiously toward the stove. She pulls her sleeves down over her wrists. I watch and wait. One spark, one wrong move, and Mina will ignite—a giant fireball through our house. But instead, Mina slides into the chair across from me.

Mom just dishes up the eggs and bacon and toast on three plates and sits with us at the table. My stomach grumbles, but I'm nervous. I want to get up from the table so bad, but I force myself to stay still. Mom's moved the flowers to the counter, so now I can't even pretend that Mina's not right there in front of me.

"Eating all this is going to make me late for school," Mina

says. She frowns and lifts up one of her pieces of bacon with a fork, like Mom's hidden something beneath it.

"I've talked to school," Mom explains, spearing a bit of egg. "Your guidance counselors know. They'll understand if you're late. I know that this is hard for you."

Mina's eyes are pink and watery and maybe about to cry, but she takes a bite. "I don't want to eat all this toast. You've made too much. It's practically slathered in butter."

"You need to eat all the toast," Mom says.

And Mina does. I'm certain that by the time she eats her last bite of eggs they have to be cold for as long as it took. But the whole plate of food is gone. She sets down her fork. She's managed not to cry. "Did I do good?"

Mom squeezes her hand. "You did." I want her to tell me that I did good, too.

Mina's schedule is different now. It's posted on the fridge along with her meal plan and a magnet with the Pinehurst emergency numbers.

From 8:00–12:00 Mina goes to regular high school. Then from 12:00–3:00 she does outpatient at Pinehurst, and then from 3:00–4:00 she'll meet with Dr. Oliver. Mom says we'll still meet with her, too, on Wednesdays. That hasn't changed. I guess I kind of thought we'd stop when Mina came home.

"Still more work to do," Mom says. I thought she'd meant

Mina, but I actually think she means us.

Mina was right about school—she's late and Mom's late and I'm late. Mom walks me into the front office and talks in soft voices with the secretary, Mrs. Rosencrantz, who then looks at me with this soft face and sorry eyes. I know they're talking about Mina. It makes me the littlest bit mad. School's the one place I could just be Em Murphy, not Emily Murphy with the sick older sister.

"I'm going to go to Science class now," I announce in a loud voice.

"Sure, honey," Mrs. Rosencrantz says, and she fills out a pass for me. The box for excused absence is checked. That makes me a little madder. Excused absences are for things like trips to the orthodontist and well checks, not because your breakfast went long. I don't want anyone doing me any favors.

Mom gives me a kiss on my forehead good-bye.

I hope she'll leave, but when I turn around I can still see her talking with Mrs. Rosencrantz through the large glass window.

Anita and Sara are talking quietly at our table when I get into Science class.

"Show her," Anita says and nudges Sara on the shoulder. Sara pushes a flyer my direction.

"What is this?" I ask. I slide into my seat and pick it up. "Do YOU have what it takes to be a Junior Roosevelt?" There's a photo of a bunch of girls with their arms around each other. They're wearing navy blue leotards and hair sparkles.

"It's the school dance squad," Anita says, her eyes big. "I thought we could all try out together. I was just telling Sara how good you were at the bowling alley."

"Really?" I blush, pleased. "But that was just a game."

"A dance game you were immediately great at. Besides, you said you took lessons."

"That was a while ago."

"That doesn't matter," Sara says. She motions in the air with her hand like she's waving away my excuses. "Look. It says they'll teach you the dance. They're running some clinics after school. And they're going to post it on YouTube." In her notebook, I can see she's sketched a picture of me and Anita and her in some kind of dance line. She's colored in our headbands with sparkly purple gel pen so they match.

"It would be so fun!" Anita adds. They both look at me expectantly.

I turn it over in my mind. I think of Dr. Franklinton-Morehouse and the After Emily.

"I'll think about it," I say. I fold the flyer up and put it in my pocket.

THINGS TO NOTICE

Hector arrives five minutes before eleven on Sunday.

I'm at our house instead of Dad's house. Dad said he thought it would be better for me to spend some time with Mina. I just think he doesn't want any reminders of everything that went so wrong at the dinner.

I watch Hector out the peephole of the front door. He's got his book bag and a plate of cookies wrapped in green plastic wrap and what looks like the brand new Unicorn Chronicles/Robots of Doom super special tucked under his arm. I think his dad's still in the driveway, because Hector keeps motioning for him to leave.

I open the door. Bean shoves her head into the space

between my knee and the door.

"Whoa." Hector jumps back. "You've got a dog."

"We've got a Bean. Are you afraid of dogs?" I ask, curious.

"No," he huffs. Still, he takes a cautious step forward. "I was just surprised by it. We only have hermit crabs." I take Bean by the collar and guide her out of the way. She's wagging her tail hard now. Hector waves one final time to his dad and comes in.

"What are their names?"

"Who?" Hector's distracted. He's still eyeing Bean and taking little side steps to the left. Bean's totally oblivious and doing her best to sniff his jeans.

"The crabs."

"Oh. Nightshade and Starlight. Not as cool as unicorns but close, maybe. Hey, here's something. Did you know when they need a bigger shell home, they actually measure other shells?" He shoves the cookies in my direction so he can act it out. He raises his arms like he's going to give me a hug. I step back. He encircles the air. "Just like that. I saw it once. It was awesome. Nightshade tried all the shells to find the best fit."

I have to admit, it is really cool.

"It would be dangerous, too," he says. "Out in the wild, since they don't have their old shells on when they're finding new ones, they're super vulnerable." Hector gestures to the cookies. "Mom said I should bring something."

Hector's mom seems like a good person already. I lift the plastic off and sniff them. "Ooh, snickerdoodles."

"Ha, that's funny," Hector says. He chuckles to himself. I brush off my face just in case I've given myself a sugar and cinnamon nose.

"What?"

"Anita does that, too. Smells things. Sometimes she'll come up to my food and say, 'I just want to smell it.' Why not just taste it?"

"Yeah." We both stand there for a minute, because it's kind of weird, I think. Us being here in my hallway instead of in Ms. Arnold's classroom—talking about hermit crab homes and smelling things instead of regular old school topics.

"We can set up at the kitchen table," I say. "My mom cleared everything off it so we could work."

Hector walks the hallway slowly, taking in the old-fashioned striped wallpaper and the thin table shoved up against the wall with its old books and old vases and fake flowers that are supposed to look real. "This is a cool house," he says.

"It's an old house," I say, rubbing the little bit of dust that's collected off one of the petals. "Some of the stuff doesn't work. Like this light switch." I flip it on and off. Nothing happens. "Mom says it's character, but sometimes that's just code for broken."

"Any secret passageways?" He bends down like he's checking.

"No," I say. I don't tell him that I've already combed every inch of the house hoping for one.

"I mean, it just would have been awesome—like *Nightshade and the Vanishing*—"

"*Violin*." We finish the sentence at the same time. My face reddens. "Well, anyway," I say, "here's the kitchen. And this is the table." Like he can't already see those things for himself.

I have my stuff set up: notebook, pens, and highlighters. I am ready to work.

Hector sits down—well, not really sits; more like he's got one leg propped up under him like a spring. He pulls out the project sheet from his binder. "Okay, so, movement!"

He says it so enthusiastically, so like Ms. Arnold, that I have to laugh. His cheeks darken.

I open up to a fresh piece of notebook paper. "We could do something with dance," I say. "Or transportation. What other things move?"

"Trains. Westward expansion. You know, like when they had the gold rush. Cars. Or maybe Henry Ford—he moved things forward, right? The assembly line and all that. Or something with sports. Like the science of throwing a ball."

I draw a web with movement in the center circle and all our ideas spiraling off it. "Do you want me to get my laptop?

We could choose a few from the list and research them more."

"Great idea," Hector says.

I run upstairs. I'm grabbing my computer from my room when I hear the garage door open, then Mina's voice. "Hello?"

I hear Hector next. His voice is so cheerful. "Hi! I'm Hector. Emily's friend."

Friend? I turn the word over in my brain. I don't know how I feel about it. But I don't have too much time to think it over, because I'm racing down the stairs to save Hector from Mina. I don't find them in the kitchen. "Hector?" I say quietly.

"In here," comes a mumbled voice. I follow the sound.

Hector and Mina are in the dining room bent over the puzzle. Hector has one of the cookies in his hand, and he's dropping crumbs all over South America. "What is this, Emily?" Mina asks.

I think maybe she's talking about the cookie. That she's angry we've brought cookies into the house because cookies are not okay.

But Hector just says, "The world." He's very matter-of-fact about it. "These are the continents. Asia, Africa, South America . . ."

It's not the cookies she's talking about at all.

Mina laughs, big and loud. My heart pangs. I realize I haven't heard her laugh in a long time. "I know that," she says. "But what are you doing? Did you guys start this?"

"It was me and Mom," I say. "She was on one of her cleaning sprees in the basement and we found it. She thought it would be a good idea."

"Oh." Mina studies the puzzle and then me. I study her, too. This is the kind of nice, regular old conversation we used to have. "That's cool. Well, I'll let you guys get back to work. I have math to finish."

"I love math," Hector says. He reaches over and snaps a piece of Australia into place. "It was great to meet you." He turns to me after she's gone upstairs. "She was nice."

"Yeah," I say. *Right now*, I think. But I like how Hector doesn't ask about how skinny she looks or that it was weird that she was wearing a bunch of layers when it's still warm.

"So I was looking at this and suddenly I was struck with a topic."

"What? Puzzles?" I ask. "I don't think that will work."

Hector shakes he head. "No, the earth. I saw it on this TV show. Underneath the earth's surface, pretty far down, are these huge rock plates." He holds his hands out. "Sometimes they slide past each other like this." He moves his hands together; they make a swishing sound. "And sometimes they push together. It's what makes volcanoes and earthquakes and stuff."

"Like, look at this." He points to the coast of Africa. "And now this." He points to the coast of South America.

"Now move them together in your mind. See, it's like a perfect fit."

"They used to be together," I say. "But now they've moved apart."

"Everything used to be together," Hector says. "One big supercontinent. Everything's still moving, too. But really, really slow. Like as fast as your fingernails grow."

"And we can't even feel it." It's amazing actually, I think. That all this huge change is happening underneath us but we don't even think about it.

I hold my breath for a second, thinking that maybe if I just concentrate hard enough, I'll be able to feel the movement underneath my feet. But there's nothing, just the creaks of the floorboards. I think it has much more to do with the house's "character" than the shifting of the plates.

"It's a good topic. I think Ms. Arnold will like it."

"Yeah?" Hector says. He looks pleased with himself. "There should be a lot of information, too. Plenty for our report. There's an exhibit at the natural history museum, too. They have these big panels where you can move the continents themselves."

"We should go," I say out loud without thinking.

Hector's eyes pop open wide. "That would be cool. My dad works there. He's the curator. We could go anytime."

"Yeah, okay. That sounds good."

"Really?"

I nod, and I'm surprised that I actually mean it.

"Awesome," he says, smiling.

We spend the rest of the morning researching and writing down notes and eating cookies. They're not as good as Grandma Bebe's, but sometimes pretty good is good enough.

I find I don't even mind it when crumbs stick to Hector's grin.

When Hector leaves, Bean and I go up to my room. I pull out my craft stuff and text Hazel.

Emily: Do you want to come over? We could make costumes for Bean.

I hold up different pieces of fabric. "This is pretty," I say, rubbing a piece of lace between my fingertips. "We could make you a bonnet. Or one of those fancy collars queens wore. You know, the frilly ones."

I think about how regal Bean would look with her long pointy nose and sharp-angled face. I take some yellow fun foam out. It would make a perfect crown.

I text Hazel again.

Emily: ????

Hazel finally texts me ten minutes later.

Hazel: Ugh, sorry. Team dinner at Lucy's. We're going to dress up for it. What do you think?

She attaches a picture of her wearing this tight skirt and top that emphasizes that she actually has boobs. Not huge ones. But something, and I think that's what matters. Hazel looks like she could be one of Mina's friends. I still look like I'm Mina's little sister.

I close my eyes. My mind goes to the pool that summer and every summer before. Me and Hazel, each sitting in our inner tubes, holding on to each other as long as possible until we finally drift apart. I watch as she floats farther and farther away.

Emily: Cute

I can't bring myself to put an exclamation point.

She doesn't respond back. I let out this big breath that lifts the wild, little baby hairs around my forehead. I stare hard at the screen. I'm thinking of all the things Hazel might be doing instead of texting me back. All the things that are more important. I try again.

Emily: Hey, guess who came over?

Emily: Hector!

Her response is immediate.

Hazel: Why?

At first, a little thrill of satisfaction zips through me, but it goes away immediately and leaves me empty. Hector and I had a good morning and here I was talking about him, knowing that Hazel wouldn't be kind.

Hazel: Don't tell anyone. Are you guys friends? What's going on?
Emily: School project.

What I don't type: *it was fun.* What I don't type: *he was nice.*

Hazel: Oh good. LOL.

She includes this little emoji that looks like a relieved face. I wonder who she's relieved for: me or her. She doesn't text anything more.

It's quiet in my room without Hazel's loudness or the chime my phone makes when someone texts me to keep me company. And Mina's in her room, probably, catching up on math. I guess my next go-to person is an infomercial doctor. So I put in my earbuds and the next *Be the Best You* CD while I finish up Bean's crown and collar.

The music begins. "Hello, friend," Dr. Franklinton-Morehouse says. "Whatever time you're listening to this—morning, noon, or night—know that we're happy you're here. What a journey we've had so far. I hope that you are still considering things to put on your before-and-after list. As we continue forward, you may discover new and different things about yourself. That's good. You're digging even deeper into that hole we referenced at the very beginning. Now that you've made plans to redefine who you are and stretch yourself, we need to talk about the next step. That step is forgiveness.

"When we hold on to past hurts, it puts a barrier between us and other people. It does not allow our balloon much room to expand. Does this mean that we must constantly allow people to hurt us? No, of course not. What we must do, though, is understand that feeling hurt is part of life. People hurt us. We hurt them."

I think of the dinner with Dad, of Mina's harsh words for me, of the cafeteria table.

"We need to learn to be forgiven, and also, to forgive. We must understand that people are growing, just as we are."

The track ends there.

* * *

It's quiet when I go downstairs to make myself a turkey sandwich for lunch. Mom's still at work. Bean's sleeping in a sunny spot.

When I walk past the dining room to go back upstairs, though, I'm surprised to see Mina hunched over the puzzle. Deep in concentration. She doesn't even notice me. I watch her as she puts a piece into place.

PUNCTUATION DAY

Hector and I spend a lot of time working on our report over the next couple of days. First, we compile the notes we have. Then we make an outline. We also write down questions that we want to find answers to at the museum.

I think we're going to have some class time to work together today, but Ms. Arnold has a surprise. She's wearing a bright blue exclamation point on her chest.

"Good morning!" she cheers. "Today is my favorite day of the year!"

"Taco Tuesday?" Martin Morris asks.

"No." She laughs. "But that is a close second now that you bring it up. It's Punctuation Day!"

"Is that something you made up?"

"Would I do that?" She pauses. "Yes, that is absolutely something I would do. But I didn't. Punctuation Day is a real live actual thing." She presses the Smart Board clicker and different types of dancing punctuation fill the screen. "Punctuation is like the road signs of language. They tell us when to stop and when to pause, when to emote things with enthusiasm, and when to question." The way she's saying this makes it all seem very exciting.

She grabs a stack of paper circles off her desk and hands a pile out to each person at the front of the rows. "Today, you are going to figure out what kind of punctuation you are."

Hector hands me one over his shoulder.

"Take out your colored pencils," Ms. Arnold says. "I want you to decorate your circle with your particular piece of punctuation. Maybe you're an exclamation point like me. Or a comma. Or a colon."

"That's an organ," someone shouts out.

"And you, sir, are a scholar," Ms. Arnold replies. "A colon is an organ and a piece of punctuation. It's a homonym." She writes the word in marker on our Word Nerd Wall. "After you've chosen and decorated, we'll share." She shakes a tiny box. "I have some safety pins to pin our badges to our shirts."

I nibble on the end of my eraser and scan the list of punctuation marks in my Language Arts book. Maybe I'm a comma—I'm pausing while Hazel's moving fast-forward ahead with new friends and field hockey and everything.

I settle on the question mark just as Ms. Arnold asks for volunteers to share. In between Bobby Rias, who's a dash, and Cara Simons, who has chosen quotation marks (she really likes to talk, I think), Hector turns around to see what I've chosen.

"You're wrong," he whispers.

"What?"

"You're not a question mark."

I frown. "What am I then?"

"One of those dot-dot-dot things."

"You mean an ellipsis?" I stop coloring.

"Yeah. That thing."

"Doesn't that mean something's missing? Like the author has left something out?" I'm kind of harsh whispering now because maybe the ellipsis is the insult of the punctuation world.

"Well, yeah." His words come out quick. "But that's not what I mean. You know, when they're at the end of a sentence. When there's more to it." He's blushing now. His ears are turning red. "More to find out. In a good way. That's you."

The bell rings and I pin my badge on like the other kids because there isn't time to change it. But I think about Hector's words all day.

When I get home, I dig through the art supplies at the bottom of my closet and pull out a spare piece of poster board. I sit on the floor and trace around the badge I've pulled from my backpack. I'm making a new one. With my gel pens, I draw three big dots in a row.

I cut it out and tack it up to my bulletin board next to my calendar and the postcard Hazel sent me last summer from New Mexico. I stare at it for a second and then I unzip the front pocket of my book bag and take out the flyer Sara and Anita gave me. I unfold it carefully and study it. I try to picture my face in the middle of the group of smiling girls. Glitter bow in my hair. Sequined leotard.

Em Murphy, Junior Roosevelt. Could I be? I say it out loud, just to myself. I say it again. To be honest, it kind of has a nice ring to it.

I open my notebook and on the left side of the T chart I write:

More to discover.

THE GARCIAS

We have to come up with a visual aid for our report, Hector says.

Maybe a clay model of the inside of the earth, I suggest. Or a poster board. Anything that's crafty. I tell him I have lots of art supplies. Hector kind of *hmms* over it and suggests that I come over one afternoon after school. Anita overhears and seconds it. "We can practice for the Roosevelts dance tryouts," she says. "They just posted the video on YouTube!" She says it like I'm definitely trying out, even though I really haven't decided yet. But *she* can see me as Em Murphy, Junior Roosevelt, and I think that means something.

Hector crosses his arms over his chest and says, "I invited her first."

Anita laughs. "We can share."

"Hey, I'm a person," I protest, but secretly my heart swells.

That's how I end up in Hector's room. Anita stands in the door; her voice is stern. "You have till four thirty. I'm watching the clock." She turns to me. "We can dance in my room. Mom helped me push my bed aside. There's plenty of space."

Hector has all our books and notes from the project spread out on the floor, and I can tell he's getting impatient to start. But I can't stop looking at all the figures lining his bookshelves and windowsill and dresser. There have to be hundreds of them. Superheroes and dinosaurs of all different kinds. Disney characters. The entire Unicorn Chronicles collection, including Nightshade, Starlight, and their team of gnome forensic scientists. "Do you have all six of them?"

Hector nods.

I shake my head in amazement. I don't have any, but people on the Underworld boards say they are *very* rare. "Why don't you have these in boxes?"

"That wouldn't be fun," he says. "You can't play with them in boxes."

Very true, I think. I make a mental note to ask if I can

hold the Nightshade figure later. Her rainbow hair shines in the late afternoon sun. She looks the most magical right now.

I sit on the floor next to him. "So what are you thinking for our visual?"

"Food," he says.

"Food? What are we going to feed people? Pieces of the earth? Fossils?"

Hector laughs. "No, but we want to show the class how our plates move, right?"

"Right."

"So let's think—what could represent magma?"

I try to think of something thick and viscous. "Oatmeal."

"That's gross."

"I like oatmeal." It's warm and filling. "Okay, what about pudding?"

"Yes, pudding! Now you're talking. I love pudding." He writes it down in his notes. "What about the plates— something flat and movable. Also delicious." He snaps his fingers. "Candy bars!"

"Hershey's and Snickers—for the rock layers." Even though I had wanted to do something crafty with my art supplies, I do think this is really good idea. Kids cheer when Mr. K passes out Wint-O-Green Mints at the end of Social Studies on Friday. Imagine how they'll react to this.

"Brilliant." Hector makes a list on a sheet of loose leaf with little check boxes down the left side. He glances at the clock. "We still have a half hour," he says.

"Can we play with the Unicorn Chronicles figures?"

Hector grins. His eyes get kind of crinkly. Mom calls them smile lines. They're the mark of a happy person, she says. "Sure!"

Turns out, not only does Hector have the Unicorn Chronicles figures, but he also has the official underground lair system complete with the elevator cave entrance (that actually moves!) and does a spot-on voice for Disastero. It's pretty great.

Anita comes in and pulls me away right at four thirty like she promised.

She's changed into black leggings and a purple tank that's knotted at the side. A yellow sports bra peeks out underneath. I have one, too, but it's mainly because all the girls have one for gym changing purposes, not because I really need one.

"I didn't bring dancing clothes," I say, feeling sheepish.

"That's all right! I'm just trying to get into the spirit of things. What you're wearing is fine. I have the video all cued up and ready to go."

We sit together on the edge of her bed. It's cool. It's like a couch and a bed all in one. Anita calls it a day bed. I look around just like Nightshade would in this kind of situation—whether she was meeting the Sasquatch informant at Fizzy's or the cockroach king in his hideout. Be aware. Observe, she'd always say. So I do.

Beyond the day bed, which has the fluffiest pillows that feel like they're covered in real fur (but not—I asked—Anita says she's an animal activist), there are bookshelves that are stuffed full of Unicorn Chronicles books in number order and these Western adventures and nonfiction books with the most lifelike pictures on the covers. They look like they're too nice to be touched, but I think they've been read tons judging from the note-covered Post-its sticking every which way out of them.

There are posters on the wall, too. Not the Nightshade or Starlight posters in my room or the brand-new field hockey ones in Hazel's. Instead, between black-and-white photos of dancers, Anita has hung ones of astronauts. Some of them even have autographs scrawled at the bottom. And then there's a framed picture of her and Hector in these official blue uniforms at what must be space camp.

"Do you want to go into space?" I ask, studying them.

She nods. "I'm doing my project on it. I want to be the first woman on Mars. Can you see it?" And suddenly I can, even though before this moment I had no idea she was interested in outer space at all. It strikes me that people are kind of like those lollipops with Tootsie Rolls in the center— if you wait awhile, you get surprised by something awesome that sits just below the surface.

I'm not sure if that idea came from me or from Dr. Franklinton-Morehouse. Either way, it seems true and promising. I'll have to write it down.

"Are you ready now?" she asks. She's practically bouncing. She hits play on her laptop. Girls jump onto the screen one at a time. They get into position. A beat starts. Suddenly, they all start dancing in sync to the music. Sharp movements. Arms and legs and feet all in perfect rhythm. I recognize the gymnasium as ours, but it looks different. There are all these cool stage lights going. Blue and yellow and red, flashing bright. It's transformed. The girls are transformed.

At the end of the performance, there's cheering and clapping.

It's so exciting and I wasn't even there. Then words appear. "Do you have what it takes?"

I'm not sure if I do. But the video makes me want to try.

Anita clicks on another clip. In this one, there are only two girls dressed in regular workout clothes. "Hi, I'm Christine," the first girl says.

"And I'm Nora," says the second. "And we're this year's captains of the Junior Roosevelts. We're here to take you through the moves that we'll be using at tryouts. We welcome girls of any dance ability. It's important that you're able to follow choreography, but mainly we want girls who are excited with a lot of spirit. Okay. Let's get started!"

Anita sets the computer on her desk so we can still see the screen and we spread out on the carpet. "Put your feet in second position—that is hip distance apart," Christine says. I think I recognize her from the lunchroom. "Now take your right hand and push left, then out. Good. Do the same with your left hand."

Pretty soon, Anita and I are bouncing and twirling to the music in sync, just like with the game. It's harder, sure. But we get the hang of it.

"So what do you think?" she says as the last few notes fade out.

"I think it could be cool." There's something here—this being tired and sweaty; the flashing gym lights and the pumping music; this taking a chance with a new friend that feels like it might actually fit with After Em.

Anita grabs my hands. "Really cool!" She says it in a way that makes me believe it.

Hector suggests ice cream.

I think to myself that he might actually be brilliant. Anita and I lace up our sneakers and then we all tell their mom where we're headed. We find her in the kitchen, in her pajama pants still, spooning meat into tortillas and then rolling them up tight like miniature sleeping bags. The kitchen smells amazing.

"Okay! Don't ruin your appetite," she says, but she grins.

"She cooks when she's stressed," Anita says as she's closing the front door behind us.

Hector must see the puzzled look on my face. "She's a journalist," he explains. "For the *Columbus Chronicle*. She writes about crime." He pauses. "She cooks a lot."

But that's not what I'm confused about.

I'm wondering what that's like—to be calmed by food instead of stressed out about it. I picture their family dinner: Hector reciting some strange factoid about zombies, Anita dreaming about space or belonging to the Junior Roosevelts, Mrs. Garcia sharing an exciting interview she's done, and Mr. Garcia talking about his day at the museum with the dinosaurs and mummies and geologic features. Together.

I wonder if it would be weird to invite myself.

THREE THINGS

It's Friday and I'm at Dad's again.

I guess enough time has passed since the disaster dinner with Mina.

Things are a little different around here. Bits of grass have finally started to emerge in the front yard, so it doesn't look *quite* so terrible. Alice has put more paint samples on the dresser because she hasn't quite sensed that the problem is not with the colors. There's a new spread on the bed, too. Before I roll out my sleeping bag on the floor, I run my hand over the comforter. Flowery. Different from my one at home, which is pink with unicorns. This one's soft and kind of pretty.

I feel guilty even liking it a little bit.

"Button," Dad yells up. "Come on down! I have a surprise for you!"

I hadn't even heard the garage door open. I'm trying to do a reread of books one-through-six before the movie premiere and I was on the part in *Nightshade and the Secret of Sasquatch Grove* where Nightshade first finds the hidden kingdom. I was totally sucked into it even though I've read it a bunch of times before. I set the book down on my sleeping bag like a tent.

"I'm in the dining room."

I can tell Dad's smiling, just from listening to his voice. I wonder what the surprise could be. Maybe he and Alice went ahead and chose the paint color for the room. That wouldn't be awesome.

Maybe it's a new bike. I still have my old one I got when I was seven. It has pink and white streamers in the handlebars and noisemakers stuck on the spokes so it *click-clacks* when the wheels turn. A new bike wouldn't be so bad.

It could be crafting stuff. It would be kind of nice to have that in both houses.

When I find Dad, he's standing over the dining room table, right next to the spot where I chipped my tooth playing tag with Mina years ago. I can still see the indentation.

He's got a box. It's brand new—not like the one Mom

and I pulled out from the basement. He opens it and dumps the pieces out.

"I got us a puzzle!" he says, turning toward me, grinning expectantly.

My mouth forms a hard line.

Dad's eyebrows arch in surprise. "I know you're working on one of these at your mom's, so I thought it would be nice if you and Alice and I could work on one together here."

"You don't get it," I say, shaking my head. My voice has this awful edge to it, but I can't help myself.

"What?" Dad pleads. "Explain it to me. Please."

"You should just know," I say, and it sounds ridiculous even to me. But it's how I feel. Because when I'm an adult, I keep thinking I'll finally know the right things to say and do. And if there's no hope for Dad, then there's no hope for me.

It would mean all the work I had done with Dr. Franklinton-Morehouse was for nothing.

"Em, I can't read your mind," he says softly. "What's going on in that head of yours?"

I take a breath and look at him. "I don't want two puzzles or family bowling night or some halfhearted awful dinner," I say. The words unspool out of me fast. "I just want all of us together. Like how it used to be. Before. When Mina was okay." My words get caught in my throat. "When we were all okay."

"Oh, honey," he says. "I hear you." And even though I didn't tell him that's what I needed, he understood. He knew.

He puts his hand on my shoulder and this time I let it stay there.

"We don't have to do the puzzle," he says. "We don't have to do anything you don't want."

"Can we just watch a movie?" I whisper. Dad nods.

I wipe my nose on the back of my hand.

Dad calls Alice and tells her there's been a change of plans.

We watch a movie on this gigantic projector screen in the basement. It's called *Clue* and it's a murder mystery story. I guess it's based on the board game. It's old and the characters are a bit ridiculous, but it makes me laugh and that feels good.

Alice can actually do a really good impression of one of the characters, Mrs. White.

After the credits roll, I don't quite feel like going to bed yet. It's actually cozy on the couch between Dad and Alice.

"Let's play a game," I say. "It's called Three Things." I've only ever played it with Hazel, but there has to be a first time for everything, I think.

"All right, Em," Dad says. "How do we play?"

"Normally, we'd pick a category and we'd each say three things about us in that category. Like, things I'm afraid of:

centipedes, Hazel's basement, and being lost out in space. But maybe I'll just name a category and we can each say one thing. Because it's late."

"That sounds fun." Alice smiles at me encouragingly. I find myself smiling back.

I rack my brain for a topic. "Okay. A fact about you that nobody knows."

"Ooh!" Alice raises her hand like she's in class. "I'll go first. I was in the spelling bee. Wait, does that count? I guess some people know that."

"It counts," I say. "I didn't know that."

Dad laughs. "Me neither. Like your school one?"

"And then the district one. I got out on *onomatopoeia*. So that means, I forever remember how to spell *onomatopoeia*." She spells it for us, standing up and everything like she's onstage. It's pretty impressive.

Then Dad goes. "I wanted to name you Aubrey."

"Really?" I say. Aubrey Murphy. It sounds so weird. Not like me at all.

"But your mom wanted to name you Emily. After Emily Brontë, the author. *Wuthering Heights* was one of her favorite books in college."

"Are you glad I'm Emily?" I ask.

"So glad," he replies. "As with most things, your mother was completely right." I wonder if me being named after a famous author is why I love books so much.

No, I'm pretty sure that's 100 percent me. But still, it's very cool.

"Your turn, Em," Alice says.

"I'm going to try out for the dance team," I blurt out. Not *I think* or *I might*. I am. "They're called the Junior Roosevelts and they get to wear sparkly outfits."

"No way!" Alice exclaims. "Hold on right here." She jumps up from the couch and runs up the stairs. She returns five minutes later with a yearbook and shoves it into my lap. "Page fifty-seven."

I flip past a bunch of girls with poofy bangs and boys with thin mustaches to a picture of a group of girls in matching pink-and-purple leotards. Sequin overload, and I love it. "Third one from the left."

It's Alice. Or kind of Alice. Her hair is big and her smile is braces-filled and too big for her face. She shrugs. "Eighth grade." I decide I like this awkward, bony, grade school Alice. If that was Before Alice, maybe After Alice is worth getting to know. Then she laughs. "I wasn't the coolest, but man, that was so fun. . . ." I can tell from the way her voice trails off that she's remembering.

"I have to do a routine to try out." I say the next part quick, before I change my mind: "Maybe you can help me."

LIFE

It's a beautiful late-September day.

It's the kind of day that still feels like summer. The teachers are letting us eat outside today. I'm wondering if it's because we're a few weeks into school and everyone's feeling a little bit stir-crazy looking out the windows. Or maybe it's because the cafeteria kind of smells like gym class and a little fresh air could do everyone good.

The reason doesn't really matter, I guess.

In the field behind school, there aren't any tables. That's good, because I get to stretch my legs out in the freshly mowed grass. It's also not good, because it's not just me and Hazel. But at least, out here, I hope there's room for all of us.

"I can't believe I have to miss your party," Gina says to Annemarie. She frowns. "I'm so bummed."

"What are you doing again?" Annemarie asks.

"Visiting my aunt," she says. "But it should be cool. She lives up in the mountains, so we'll get to go hiking and stuff." Her eyes light up. "We're going on one of the tougher trails this time."

"My dad and I've gone hiking," I say. "Have you ever gone to Hocking Hills?"

"Yes!" Gina replies. "Have you gone on the zip line?"

"Amazing—"

Annemarie frowns. "My party's going to be amazing."

Lucy waves a carrot in our direction. "We can play Truth or Dare. But dares only. And watch scary movies. I'll bring *The Shining*." I'm pretty sure that's rated R and I'm not allowed to watch it, but I keep my mouth shut. "We can watch it later when it's dark."

Annemarie just nods at all Lucy's plans, even though it's *her* birthday. "My mom's already started to get ready. Chips and doughnuts for breakfast and—"

"Vegetables, I hope," Lucy says. "You remember what Coach says."

I can't keep my mouth shut this time. "What does Coach say?"

Lucy rolls her eyes like I've just asked her to share field

hockey secrets. "We have to eat clean foods. Vegetables, fruits, lean meats." She pokes Annemarie's side with her finger. Annemarie's face flushes.

I wince. "Um, foods can't really be clean," I say, and I realize that the words coming out of my mouth are the same words that came out of Evie's at one of our sessions just a few weeks ago. "That would mean that some foods are dirty, and that's just not true. All foods are okay."

The conversation around the circle stops and everyone looks at me except for Lucy, who exchanges a glance with Hazel. Gina watches them and frowns. Hazel sets her lunch down, jumps up, and holds out her hand. "I want to tell you something real quick."

I'm confused, but I grab it anyway. She pulls me up. She walks fast, taking these long strides, and I have to jog to keep pace. When we reach the edge of the field, she turns to me. She's not happy. "Why did you have to do that?"

"Do what? What did I do?"

"Say that," she says. "About the food. We were just talking about the party, and now you've made it *really* uncomfortable."

"But it's true," I say. I lower my voice, even though there's no one around besides her to hear me. "You know about Mina."

"Yeah," she says. "But not everyone's Mina. And not

everyone knows about Mina. And sometimes people just want to have a regular conversation without you saying something dumb."

My heart stops. Time stands still. "You think I say dumb things?"

"I didn't mean it like that," Hazel says. Her cheeks redden. "But you know. I'll say something about Joey or whoever and you just want to talk about what happened in Language Arts class or the Unicorn Chronicles."

"We like that stuff."

She shrugs. "I guess I'm more interested in real life right now, you know?"

"Are you excited about the movie even?" I hate that I sound like I'm pouting.

"Em, yes!" she says. She seems exasperated, the way Mom sometimes is when I don't hear her talking to me when I'm deep inside some book. "Why are you making such a big deal about all this? We're still going to the movie. We're still going to have fun at the party. All I'm asking is for you to be normal."

She stares at me earnestly. "So, I think I'm going to sit with Lucy tomorrow. At her table. Okay."

I think *okay* is supposed to be a question. But it doesn't come out that way at all.

* * *

"Want to see a picture of my cat?" Sara asks.

I'm sitting on the concrete stairs outside school waiting for Mom to pick me up.

"Sure," I say. I'll take any distraction from thinking about what happened at lunch, what would happen at lunch tomorrow. Sara takes a seat next to me and pulls out her phone. There are doodles all over the case—monsters and robots and dogs with handlebar mustaches.

"Did you draw all that?"

She smiles sheepishly. "Yeah."

"They're really good."

"Thanks." She presses the power button and types in a password. She presses the photo icon. The most adorable picture ever pops onto the screen. It's this gray cat with a tiny white face and it's wearing a frog hat tied under its chin. Two bulging, fabric eyes stare back it me from the top of its head.

"Her name's Barbara." I love when animals have people names.

"Did you make that?" I ask, pointing at the hat.

"Yeah," she says. "Me and my sister Sasha. We made a business last summer. Cat Couture. We knitted a bunch of those and sold them door-to-door."

"Did you sell a lot?"

She laughs. "No way. There's more of a demand for

lemonade than cat clothes." She pauses, thinking. "But we did sell a few, and that's more than none."

"You could be at the start of a cat clothes revolution."

"A cat clothes empire, right here in Ohio."

"I bet you could sell them online. Put it on Instagram and stuff." I pull out my phone and scroll to the picture of Bean wearing the crown and Elizabethan collar. "I make my dog clothes, too."

"So cute! She really looks royal," Sara says, giggling.

"Thanks." Her words make me feel warm inside.

"Maybe you could come over sometime. We could use my sewing machine." I wonder if I could branch out into cat clothes. I bet Pickle would love a frog hat.

I'm putting the last piece of North America in place when Mina walks into the dining room.

"It's looking good," she says. She breaks off a piece of her granola bar and pops it into her mouth. Evie says that it's easier sometimes for Mina to eat when she has her mind on something else, like our puzzle. "Ooh." She picks up a piece from the table and fits it into Asia.

We sit there for a minute, studying the pieces. Every few seconds, I glance over at my cell phone that I've laid down faceup next to me so I can see it.

"Technology addiction is real, Em," Mina says. "You kids

are always on Snapchat or ChattyCat or FishTalk. . . ."

"I don't think most of those are actually real. And you *are* a kid. Technically."

Mina laughs, the same big laugh she did that day with Hector. "I *know*. And I'm a teen. Technically. But for real, why do you keep looking at it? You interested in that kid who came over? What was his name? Henry?"

"Hector. And he's just my friend."

Mina elbows my arm. "All I'm saying is that he's cute. Not for me, of course. But for a fellow twelve-year-old."

"Mina!"

"So if it's not Hector"—she makes her voice all throaty—"then who?"

I sigh. What I want to tell her is that I'm waiting for Hazel to text me. To say that she's sorry and she didn't mean the things she said to me today outside at lunch. But that would mean explaining what I had said about food and stuff, and I don't want to do that.

Instead I say, "It's confusing."

"What is?"

"Life."

Mina nods thoughtfully. "Yeah. Yeah it is."

I never get a text from Hazel that night, but I do get one from Anita to me and an unknown number. It's the emoji with the two dancing girls dressed in black leotards.

"Tryouts are SO soon!" she adds. Then she texts a few more exclamation points for good measure.

The unknown number texts the emoji of the salsa girl in the red dress.

I figure it must be Sara. I add her to my phone.

CAFETERIA ADVENTURES: UNCENSORED

'd bring a knife," Lloyd says as I sit down at the lunch table—my new table for the past four days. It's me and Lloyd and Hector—Sara and Anita have second lunch. Lloyd says that it's okay: good things come in threes. Three Musketeers. Three blind mice. The Three Stooges. I have to say, it's an interesting theory. I watch as he takes celery sticks from a Ziploc bag and dips them in ranch one at a time. He's dipping his sleeve in, too.

"A knife? Can you say that at school?" I whisper. I look around for Mustard Tie, aka Mr. Georges, but he's halfway across the cafeteria waving a crumpled-up napkin in the air in this really stern way. Someone probably threw it.

"Sure. I'm not bringing it *to* school. That would be dumb. I'm bringing it to the island."

"What island?"

"The one on *Island Adventures: Uncensored*. You know, the show?"

"Haven't seen it."

"Channel twenty-two. Eight thirty. Tonight," Hector says, setting his lunch tray down. He's grinning. "You've got to see it. They run around and try to survive on this wild island for twenty-one days with no clothes on."

"No way!" I say. I shake my head. "Do you *see* anything?" I cannot even imagine it. I do not want to. I resist the urge to cover my eyes, even though there's no TV in front of me.

Lloyd slaps his knee and howls. A few kids at the table next to us look over. He doesn't seem to mind. "Of course not. It's television."

"Why no clothes then? That's weird."

"It's hard-core," Hector replies. "Like the cavemen."

"Or cavewoman," I add. "Cave people."

"Sure. Cave people." To Lloyd he says, "Did you see the episode with the wild boar? That one was awesomesauce."

"Well, what would you bring?" I ask.

"Fire starter," Hector says. "It gets cold there at night and you can't drink the water unless you boil it."

"But that's not authentic," Lloyd says. "That's not

something a caveman would use." I get the sense that he's thought a lot about this.

"Is a knife?" I ask.

"More than a fire starter," he replies. "Brilliant idea alert. You guys should do this for your project."

"What does it have to do with movement?" Hector asks.

Lloyd shrugs. "It doesn't. But it would be cool."

"Our project is already cool," Hector says. "The coolest."

"What are you doing?" Lloyd asks.

"Top secret," I reply.

Lloyd rolls his eyes. "What would you take, Em?"

I need only a second to think about it. "Clothes."

They both groan, but frankly, I'd think they'd miss their own if they were stranded on that island. I wonder what Hazel would choose, but when I look over, she and Lucy are whispering. Their heads practically touch. She doesn't even glance my way.

At eight thirty, Mina finds me and Bean in front of the TV.

"Em, what is this?" she asks, once she sees the screen. She tries to grab the remote out of my hand. "Does Mom know you're watching this?"

I laugh and wave her away. "It's *Island Adventure: Uncensored*. Those people have to survive on it for twenty-one days."

Her jaw drops. "Without clothes?"

I'm kind of pleased that Mina had the exact same reaction as me. "I *know*!"

Mina flops down on the couch and curls her feet underneath her bottom. Only Bean's in between us. We're a Bean sandwich.

At the end of the hour, Mina turns to me. "Huh," she says, shaking her head in wonder. "That was actually pretty good." We decide to watch another episode.

SCHOOL PICTURE DAY

Posters advertising school picture day start to appear in the hallways.

Each poster features a different kid. Some are wearing scarves around their necks. Others are in colorful, long-sleeve T-shirts. They pose different ways—hands on their hips or heads tilted to the side. All the kids wear big, toothy grins to go with their perfect hair. Between Math and Science class one morning, I study the one near my locker.

There are kids streaming all around me. They're loud and bumpy, but I stand firm. All my focus goes to the words underneath the photograph. *Be the best you*, it reads, *on your school picture day!*

I feel like the words are a sign.

* * *

"What are you doing?" Mina asks. She's standing in the doorway of my room leaning against the frame. She has her Pinehurst journal in her hand and is still wearing her jacket. She must have just gotten home from group. Me, I'm laying out every piece of clothing I have (except for my first-day-of-school outfit, which will remain balled up in the back of my closet) on the bed and the floor because I've run out of room.

I let out a deep sigh. "Picture day's tomorrow. I have nothing to wear."

"It looks like you have lots to wear," she says, surveying the clothes and Bean, who has made a comfy nest on a pile of discards.

"I guess. But not the right things."

"Come on," she says. She leaves the door and I hesitate, unsure.

"Are you coming?" she calls.

"Yeah, okay," I say. I follow her into her room. It's the first time I've been in there since she got home. Mom's vacuum lines have all been stepped over, and there's a little more dust than usual. Still, Mina's a neat person. Her schoolbooks are in an orderly pile on her desk. She has a new picture of her and Phoebs tacked up on her bulletin board. Dirty laundry is piling up in her hamper.

The room looks lived in. It's a good feeling.

She pats the bed. I sit down and she opens her closet. She hums, riffling through hangers. She occasionally pulls something out—a long-sleeved blouse or a sweater—shakes her head, and puts it back. "Okay, try this on," she says. She holds up a white, short-sleeved top with a glittery navy blue collar.

"Ooh, I love glitter," I say.

"I know." She pulls out some slim navy blue pants. "What about these together?" I nod but I really have no idea. I think they look good together, but that's why I need her now and why I needed her that day at the mall.

I take them both into my room and slip out of my unicorn shirt and jeans I wore to school today. I slip the shirt over my head and button the clasp at the back of the collar. The pants are a little snug, but maybe they're supposed to be. I'm not used to the way they cling to my legs.

"What do you think?" I ask, going back into Mina's room. Mina adjusts the bottom of the shirt and taps her cheek with her finger. She goes to her jewelry box and pulls out two of the sparkliest earrings. They're just studs but they're so pretty. They catch the light. I put them in.

"Perfect," Mina says. "But we need a fashion show."

"A fashion show?"

"Yeah, in the hallway. I mean runway." And just like that, it's me and Old Mina. Making over our dolls. Doing fashion shows in the hallway. Playing dress-up in ridiculous outfits. "I'll put on some music."

"You do it, too," I say. I'm feeling giddy now.

"Okay," Mina says. "I can do your hair tomorrow morning. Big and curly with the round brush." I picture how that will look. Very fancy-pants. Like a movie star maybe, or at least one of the models in *Teen Scene*. "There's some product in the bathroom we can use."

I walk out into the hallway and practice my fashion show moves. I strut down the length of the carpet runner, put my hand on my hip, and twirl. The outfit feels a little bit like magic, and the fact that Mina picked it out makes it even better. Bean sashays all the way back with me. She's a natural.

Mina's taking a while to get dressed, so I peek my head in the door. She's standing in front of her closet mirror and pulling at the waist of a skirt she's slipped on.

"Are you ready?"

She doesn't look at me. "I don't think it used to fit like this." She rubs her hands down the length of it, hard, like maybe she could remove the fabric. Her hand moves back up to her stomach. She shifts in the skirt uncomfortably. "Does it look tight? It feels tight." She takes a shaky breath in.

"Mina, no." It just looks normal to me. I try to sound confident. But I can tell she doesn't believe me. A giant fist begins to squeeze my chest tight. "No, it looks good. Great, even. It looks great." The words tumble out quick. The expression on Mina's face doesn't change. "Bean's waiting for us in the hallway. The fashion show." I'm desperate to remind her.

Mina looks at me and shakes her head. She puts her hand on her cheek. "I can't right now." Just like that, it's as if a shade has been drawn over her face. The moment is over. "But you look great, Em. Best picture day ever."

"Best picture day ever," I say in a soft voice.

I go back to my room and put away all the clothes I had gotten out. I carefully take off Mina's outfit and hang it up on the doorknob of my closet. Ready for tomorrow.

When I go to see if Mina's okay, her door is closed.

The next morning, I'm standing in front of Mina's door again with the round brush and hair dryer and the product stuff she mentioned. It looks like putty and smells refreshing, like peaches. My hair, damp from the shower, hangs straight down. I wear a bath towel around my shoulders like a cape. I don't want to get Mina's shirt wet. I'm wearing her favorite earrings. I like how they sparkle when I twist my head from side to side. I'm feeling excited.

It's still very early because I figure these things take time and I want to get a head start, but she's up, because I can see the light peeking out from under the door.

"Mina," I whisper. I don't want to wake Mom just yet, even though the hair dryer probably will in a few minutes. This is the only day she gets to sleep in a little.

I push open the door.

Mina's facing away from the door, lying down on her carpet. She doesn't see me right away, but I watch as she curls up to her knees and then back down. Up, then down. Up, then down, at this impossibly rapid pace. It takes me a minute to process. I see what she's doing but I don't fully understand.

"Mina," I say, louder this time. "What are you doing?" My breath catches.

She stops and turns to me, red-faced—from being caught, from the exertion, I don't know. "Get out." She crawls on her hands and knees to try to shut the door, but I keep it open with my foot.

"You're not supposed to be doing this." She knows it and I know it and my heart is knocking so hard in my chest that it's the only thing I hear. Mina's still sick. Mina could go away again. The thought makes my head feel suddenly woozy. I grab onto the door frame. "Mom! MOM!"

"Shut up, Emily," Mina hisses. "Just shut up. You don't understand."

"I thought you weren't doing this anymore," I whisper.

I think about yesterday and her picking out my clothes. I think about how nice it was to feel like things were exactly as they used to be. Now everything's messed up again.

"Girls," Mom says. She's emerged from her room, in her pajamas, and yawning. Her hair is still big from sleep. "What's going on?"

She fumbles with her glasses and slips them on and her eyes go wide. Somehow she knows what Mina's been doing without me having to explain. Maybe it's the tiny beads of sweat that dot Mina's forehead or that she's on the ground in her exercise clothes. "Mina, no. No."

Mina lies back down on the floor, defeated, and starts to cry. Little streams of tears run past her nose and onto the carpet. Bean runs in and starts to lick Mina's face. Mina lets her. "I'm sorry, Mommy," Mina says in this small voice. She curls up like a pill bug. "I'm so sorry. I don't know why I did it."

Mom goes to Mina and kneels down next to her. She strokes her cheek. "It's okay, sweetie. It's okay."

The hair dryer goes limp in my hand. "What about my hair?" I say. "You were supposed to do my hair."

Mom shakes her head. "Oh, Emily, not now."

"But it was important. You promised." I just needed her to do this one thing to prove that we could be okay again.

"I know," Mina says. She hiccups through her tears.

"You don't." I'm crying now, too. "You are always doing this. You're supposed to be getting better. You're supposed to not be exercising. You're supposed to do my hair." I know my hair should be the least important of all, but it doesn't feel that way.

I throw my hairbrush on the floor. "I'm sick of this. I'm so sick of this." Everything tangled up inside me is unwinding so, so fast. I'm out of control. "You're a bad sister."

Mom gasps. Mina cries harder.

"Emily!" Mom says. Her eyes are hard. "That is enough."

"No, she's right," Mina says.

I should say I'm sorry. I should comfort Mina. But my chest is so tight. "I'm never going to ask you for anything again."

I leave the brush on the floor and stomp down the hall into the bathroom. I unload the product and the hair dryer onto the counter. I look at myself in the mirror. My face is blotchy and swollen around the eyes. My almost-dry hair hangs in limp clumps. I look absolutely nothing like the image I had in my mind.

I think about *this picture* in the yearbook. I imagine trading *this picture* with friends. This is how I'll remember sixth grade forever and ever. This is not the best me at all. I cry harder.

"I don't need you," I yell.

I hear Mom talking to Mina in soft tones. I'm sure she's telling Mina that I'm the terrible one. I think about Dr. Franklinton-Morehouse. I picture him in the corner, in his chair, stroking his cat and judging me. "You aren't growing at all, Emily Murphy," he'd say. Shame and regret wash over me. I can't bear to face Mom or Mina right now, even though I hear Mom calling my name from Mina's room.

Instead, I throw my hair up in the droopiest, saddest ponytail and run out the door to try to catch the bus to school.

LIKE SISTERS

Hazel looks like one of the models on the picture day posters.

I find her outside her locker with Lucy. They're squeezed shoulder to shoulder, looking at their reflections in the tiny mirror she has hanging up, just like we did at the end of summer. Their hair hangs in smooth, flat sheets. Hazel pulls the end of one strand like she can somehow make it straighter.

They're both wearing their navy team polos and matching silver ball earrings. If you just glanced over quickly, like you had spotted something farther down the hall, you would have sworn they were sisters.

I don't stop. I don't want her to ask about my hair or my

splotchy face or talk about what happened with Mina that morning.

They don't even see me walk by.

Anita's sitting cross-legged in front of our lockers with Sara. Sara's been meeting us here the last few days even though her locker is in a completely different hallway.

Anita has bright pink ribbons woven through each of her braids, and each of Sara's braids ends in sparkly silver beads. Extra fancy. Picture day ready. They share an iPod, one earbud for each of them. "Letter M," Anita exclaims when I get closer. "Hey, wait." She taps Sara on the knee. Sara looks up, too. "Are you okay?"

I managed not to cry any on the bus, but now the tears start to well up again. I squeeze my eyes closed to try to shut them out. I could tell them about Mina and her promises and the terrible things I said, but all I can utter is "My hair."

Anita and Sara exchange a look and pop up. "Come on," Anita says. She grabs me by the hand and drags me into the girls' bathroom down the hall. There are already some girls crowded around the mirror, but Anita gives them a look and they make room.

"Squat down a little," Anita says. "We can fix this."

Sara hands me my ponytail holder and they both examine my hair like I'm on one of those reality makeover shows.

Anita runs her hands through it. "We could do a fishtail braid," she says thoughtfully. "Or a lobster tail. That might be pretty easy."

"Hmm...," Sara says. She grabs a front strand and starts twisting it around two others in a circular motion. "What about a crown braid."

Anita steps back and taps her finger on her lips. "Perfect. Okay, be right back." She rushes out the bathroom door.

By now, the other girls have left, too. "So did you wake up late or something?" Sara says. Her tongue is sticking out between her teeth in concentration.

"No. My sister was supposed to do it and then she couldn't."

"I'm sorry," she says. And she sounds like she really means it.

I hesitate, wondering how much to say, but I'm just so tired of holding things in. "She's sick. My sister, that is. She was in the hospital for a while and now she's back."

"Is she better?"

I let out a soft breath. *Is* she better? "I guess. I don't know. I thought she was, but—" I don't finish my sentence.

Sara stops braiding for a second. Her sad eyes meet mine in the mirror. "That stinks."

"Yeah. It really does."

"You're good at this," I say after a moment, watching as

her fingers start twisting and pulling my hair again.

She laughs a little. "I have four sisters. I have to be." She thinks I'm talking about the braiding, and she is good. But I'm also talking about the way she knows the right thing to say. Sara's good at being a friend. "I learned from Sasha—the cat business sister. She's the oldest. And then there's Sammy and Vonnie."

"You're all *S* names but one?"

"Vonnie's short for Siobhan," she says. "It gets confusing."

The bathroom door swings open. Anita's holding up two things in her hands triumphantly. "It took some asking around, but I've found it," she says. She stands in front of the mirror facing me and opens a compact. "I borrowed this from Penny." She dabs a circular puff in some powder. "Close your eyes." She brushes it lightly over my face. "Okay, open." My face still looks a little red, but to be honest, it looks *a lot* better. Smoothed out and more bubblegum than fire engine.

"Hand me your hair tie," Sara says. I do and she wraps it around the end of the braid. Then she tucks it under a clump of hair on the back of my head. "It shows off your sparkly earrings." They shimmer in the two fluorescent bathroom lights that are working. "Pretty."

"Now pucker your lips," Anita says. She demonstrates. She brushes a light pink shade onto my mouth. It's not

Very Berry, but it somehow fits me better.

"What is it?" I ask.

Anita turns the lip gloss tube over. "Cotton Candy Dream," she says.

We look in the mirror, me sandwiched in between. We don't look anything alike, but we're all wearing braids and have the same slightly silly smiles. I can't help but think that maybe, in this moment, we kind of look like sisters, too.

They call us down in previously assigned groups for pictures. They name each one after a different value or characteristic Eleanor Roosevelt had, like perseverance or fortitude. I think they figure if we hear the words enough, maybe they'll sink in.

My group is called during Language Arts. Ms. Arnold's in the middle of talking about the wonderful world of independent and dependent clauses, so it's actually an okay time to go. "Will anyone in the Respect group please report to the gymnasium for pictures? Thank you," comes the announcement over the loudspeaker.

Hector and I and a few other kids head down the hall.

The photographer stands at the doorway, collecting our money envelopes. "Height order," he says. "Shortest to tallest." I guess so they only have to adjust the camera a few times.

A teacher monitors the line. Kids are standing back-to-back, comparing heights. I start to head toward the back because I already know I'm one of the tallest kids. Hector hesitates.

"Don't be shy," the teacher says, gesturing at Hector. "Shorter kids in the front."

Joey Peters nudges elbows with another spiky-haired boy. He tilts his head in Hector's direction. They both snicker.

The teacher claps her hands. She didn't see. "The quicker we get in line, the quicker we get back to class." That doesn't motivate many people.

Over the noise, someone coughs "Shrimp" into their hand. Or maybe it's "Soap."

Hector doesn't hear. Or maybe he pretends not to hear. But I think he does, because I watch his cheeks darken.

"Doesn't it bother you?" I ask before I can stop myself.

"What?" Hector asks.

"What those kids said. About you being a shrimp or whatever." And now I'm feeling terrible because maybe Hector really *didn't* hear them.

Hector smiles ruefully. "I *am* short. Can't hide it."

"But when people say stuff . . ." I'm not quite sure how to finish.

He shrugs. "Lots of people say stuff. Mom says you can't let it get to you. People write her all the time about her articles. Ridiculous stuff. She says it's easy to say things. It's harder to say something that matters. Those are the words you let in. Like, what do you think?"

"About what?"

"About me."

His question takes me by surprise. I take a minute. Finally I say, "You're nice and know a bunch of random stuff and are good at coming up with project ideas." I grin. "And you like great books. And those snickerdoodles you brought over were super yummy."

"Really?" Hector says. He shoves his hands into his jeans pockets.

"Yeah."

His smile grows bigger. "Cool."

The teacher's getting more frantic now because most of the kids are still milling around. "You, go," she says, gesturing for me to move to the back of the line.

Hector gives me a salute and walks up to the front of the line, not even glancing at Joey Peters or the spiky-haired boy.

I take my place, when Avery Williams from math class taps me on the shoulder. "We need to switch," she says. "You're a little bit taller."

"I don't think—"

"Stand back-to-back with me," she says. I do and her hand hits the back of my head, just underneath my braid. She steps in front of me.

Hector and I are on the very outside of the group.

I'm the last one to get my picture taken. Hector waits for me by the door. On the way back to class, he tells me about a cool book his dad brought home for our project. It has a lot of great pictures we could show the class, he says.

I am barely listening, though, because now all I can think about is what I said to Mina that morning.

A PHONE CALL

I take the Pinehurst magnet into my room when I get home and close the door, even though no one else is home.

I figure I have fifteen, maybe thirty minutes to call Evie. I have to time it perfectly to make sure that it's after Mina leaves Pinehurst but before she walks in the front door. I watch the horn on my unicorn clock spin round and round.

I already have the number keyed in when the clock turns 4:05. I figure I'm okay. It rings once. Twice.

"Pinehurst Residential Treatment Facility," a receptionist says. "How may I direct your call?"

"I'd like to speak with Dr. Evie Oliver," I say. I wipe my hands on Mina's pants that I'm still wearing. I've been rehearsing what I'm going to say all day long.

"I can put you through to her voicemail box if that's okay." That won't do. What if she calls back when Mina is home?

"No. No, that's not okay. I need to talk to her right now."

The receptionist's voice takes on more urgency. "Is this an emergency? Do you need help?"

"No, no. It's not an emergency. But I do need to talk with her. Please tell her it's Em Murphy. Mina Murphy's sister."

"All right, hon," the receptionist says. "Please hold. I'll see what I can do."

There're some gentle sounds. Crickets. Birds chirping. A babbling brook. It should be calming, but all it makes me feel is itchy and nervous, like I'm stuck out in nature.

I hear a click on the line and I know Evie's there. I don't even wait until she says hello. "You said it was supposed to be a mountain and I understand that mountains are hard to climb but this morning was really, really horrible. And Mina promised she'd do my hair but then she couldn't and didn't. I was so, so mad and I said terrible things." I take a breath. "I said she was a bad sister and now I'm afraid she's going to die and that the last thing she'll remember is that I said that about her."

I pause. Tears are streaming down my face now. "Is Mina going to die?"

"Emily, Emily." Evie's voice sounds so kind it makes me cry harder. "We can't tell what the future holds, but we hope not. We hope that Mina's going to be okay. She's really working hard, but the truth is recovery can take years. And yes, it's a mountain, but mountains have peaks and valleys. It's not a straight path. Does that make sense?"

"Yeah," I say in a small voice.

"And you've got to be gentle—"

"I know, I have to be gentle with Mina."

"With yourself, Emily. This is not an easy thing. It's okay to get angry or frustrated sometimes. You said what you did because you love her and want her to get better. I hope that maybe you'll talk about some of these feelings at our next family session. Do you think you might be able to do that?"

"Maybe."

NATURAL HISTORY MUSEUM

"We meet again," Dr. Franklinton-Morehouse says. "I'm so glad you're here. It's always nice to have others on the journey with us. I hope you've stretched yourself. I hope you're changing the shape of who you are, redefining yourself.

"Now, I want us to start thinking outside ourselves. So many times, when we start thinking about our interior growth, we forget the people on the outside. For your next challenge, I want you to surprise someone special. This will feel good, yes. But it will also help reinforce the fact that you, too, can cause change. You can impact the life of someone else in a positive way."

In my notebook, I write down the people in my life who I could surprise:

Mom

Dad

Ms. Arnold

Hector

Anita

I write Mina's name down underneath all of them. I circle it and I cross it out. It's been days since the hair incident.

I lie back on my pillow and look at the ceiling until it's time for Dad to drop me off to meet Hector at the museum.

In the car, Dad's tapping his hands against the steering wheel to the beat of the music again. I'm thinking maybe he should've been a drummer. Maybe for the next midlife crisis.

When we slow to a stop at a red light, he turns the music down.

"So, Button." He turns to me with soft eyes. "I heard you and Mina got in a fight."

I grip the notebook in my lap harder. "From who? Mom?"

"Yeah, Mom."

"I didn't know you guys talked so much."

"Of course we do. We're your parents." He takes a deep breath. "I think you should talk to Mina."

I frown. I know I need to. There're a thousand things I want to say to her. I'm sorry and I'm terrible and can we start over? But the words seem to lock up tight whenever I see her at dinner or in the bathroom, and the hurt feels fresh all over again. "I think you need to talk to her, too."

"I know." The light turns green, so Dad can't look at me, but even from the side I can tell his eyes are wet. "I messed up. I really messed up. I guess, I don't know. This is dumb thinking, but I guess I thought that maybe I was to blame for all of it and it would be better if I just stayed away."

"Really?"

"And—" There's a tear trailing down his cheek now. He brushes it away roughly with the back of his hand. I don't remember the last time I saw him cry. "It was just awful to see her so sick. I didn't want to face it. I didn't want to think about what could happen. And maybe that's why I came on so strong with the bowling and everything. I didn't want to lose both my girls."

"You haven't lost Mina," I say. "Or me." I reach out and pat his hand gingerly with my own. "You could call her. You could come on Wednesday with Evie—she's actually really smart and helpful." I think about how kind she was on the phone to me, and my eyes start to sting. "You could invite Mina to bowling night."

"You still want to do bowling night?" He's hopeful.

I shrug. "Sure. If's Mina's there. And we don't call ourselves the Turkeys."

Dad laughs. "I think that name's taken anyways."

It's still early Saturday morning, so the museum isn't crowded at all. Dad drops me off at the front and gives me a kiss good-bye on the forehead. "You're a smart kid, Button." I pretend to wipe it off but grin. He waves to Hector and his dad, who are already there waiting.

We follow Hector's dad through the special employee entrance. The security guard greets him. "Hey there, Dr. Garcia. I see you've got two visitors today."

"I didn't know your dad was a doctor," I whisper.

"Just a history one," Hector whispers back.

Dr. Garcia sounds pretty fancy and important. He puts his hand on Hector's shoulder. "Ed, you remember my son Hector. And this is his friend Emily. They're researching for a school project. They're going to check out the Earth History exhibit."

"Well, this is the place to be." Ed prints off two special passes with our names on them. We stick them to our shirts. "Be sure to check out the dinosaurs, too. They're my favorite."

Hector's dad tells us that he's going to work a little in his office but we can meet him in the food pavilion at eleven o'clock for lunch.

What's especially cool about this museum is that it used to be a train station, so the lobby is huge with really high ceilings. There are these colorful painted murals at the top showing the history of America. Hector grabs a map from the visitor center sign.

"There's a book where kids live in a museum," he says, unfolding it. I think Hector has an interesting fact for just about everything.

"This museum?"

"No, the Met in New York. It's an art museum. They hide in the bathrooms and go on tours with school groups and take baths in the fountains. Wouldn't that be awesome? To live here and learn cool things. I bet you could sleep in the dinosaur exhibit."

"What happens in the end? To the kids," I say.

Hector grins. "You need to read it."

"I won't read it."

He shrugs. "Then you'll never know."

I groan, but I follow him down a long winding corridor to a huge sign that says *Earth History*, complete with volcanoes and mountains that look like they're rising up out of the wood. I unzip my backpack and pull out my notebook and pen. I flip to an empty page.

The exhibit is set up chronologically and starts at the beginning, like you've traveled back in time to the very earliest days of earth. There are written signs and gigantic picture panels that have movable parts or light-up components where you can answer questions about what you just learned.

I take a lot of notes because everything is pretty fascinating:

EARTH HISTORY

Earth used to be made of lava and was pretty much a giant volcano.

We could not have breathed in early atmosphere. (Eek!)

Earth is 4.5 billion years old.

Earth change is always happening! Evolution of animals (simple, one-celled to us; extinction), continents moved around because of shifting plates.

I stop when I get to the display that says *Plate Tectonics* at the top. Hector's already there. He's pressing the button that shows the movement of the continents. Every time he presses it, the glowing continents appear to move—going from one giant landmass to where they are today. There's a section called *Evidence*, too. It has a little detective and magnifying glass at the top.

Similar rocks found in western Africa and eastern South America

Fossils in Australia just like fossils in South Asia (same plants?)

It's proof that change has taken place.

It's almost eleven and time to meet Hector's dad for lunch, but we take a detour through the dinosaur exhibit.

When you walk through it, you feel like you've traveled back in time.

Huge lifelike creatures rise up so high that their heads almost clip the ceiling. There are smaller dinosaurs, too. All kinds of land and water creatures. Plants. Mist. It's like a diorama come to life. Small metal plaques surround the exhibit. Some of the names I recognize: triceratops and stegosaurus. But that's just because Mina and I totally wore out our *Land Before Time* DVD when we were younger. I don't think it's the best source of scientific knowledge or anything.

I always wanted to be Ducky, who was this cheerful green dinosaur. Mina would pretend to be Littlefoot. I'm thinking about this when I say, "What dinosaur would you be?" to Hector, who's examining a dinosaur footprint housed in a glass case.

"The Troodon," he says. He doesn't even have to think

about it. He walks around the exhibit and I follow him. He stops in front of a small dinosaur perched on two legs in the middle of a patch of realistic-looking fake grass. There's a picture next to it, showing that this dinosaur was even smaller than a regular-sized human. "He had a big brain. Smart, but he was fierce. Like me." He grins. "You get a bunch of Troodons together? You better watch out."

Hector's dad meets us in the food pavilion, which is a fancy name for cafeteria, but it's nicer than the school one. Hector and I both get a cheeseburger and milk shake. Hector's dad tells us all about an exhibit that's coming in a few weeks: mummies. He's very animated talking about a bunch of preserved dead guys. I can see where Hector gets his expert voice.

On the way out, we stop in the gift shop. While Hector looks at the geodes and fossils, I look at the miniature dinosaurs. I find one that looks like the Troodon. The lady at the register rings me up and wraps it in white tissue.

I hide it away in my bag.

MOVIE TIME 8

Movie day has finally arrived!

I'm waiting on the porch because Mina's over at Phoebe's and Mom's at work. My feet tap out a rhythm on the concrete; I can't seem to keep them still. It keeps me busy anyway. Busy so I can ignore the nervous feeling that's joined the excited one in my stomach.

Hazel wants me to come. Even with everything that's happened. I know this because she texted me with details. I'm invited. I take a deep breath in. Annemarie and Lucy and Hazel want me to come. That's what I tell myself.

My sleeping bag and pillow are at my feet. Bean's favorite stuffed rabbit is tucked deep down in my duffel beneath my pj's and toothbrush. No one can see him, but I'll know he's there. Bean's watching me, making nose prints on the front window. Every time I turn around, her tail wags.

A car slows down in front of our house and then pulls into our driveway. I give a little wave, but the only one who waves back is Annemarie's mom. She jumps out. She has the same springy hair and pointy chin as Annemarie but is much more smiley.

"Emily," she says. "I'm so glad you are able to join us. The girls are so excited for the movie."

She takes my stuff and puts it into the trunk on top of Hazel's and Lucy's things that are already in there. Their duffels are navy and white with two little field hockey sticks crossing over the front. My yellow one just kind of sits there like an odd little duck.

The three girls are already in the back—Hazel tucked in between Annemarie and Lucy—so I slide into the front passenger seat. I sit there quietly till we pull out of the driveway, feeling like I've walked into a party already happening. I take a deep breath and try to relax. This will be fine. Fun. I will be normal. This will be fun. "Happy birthday, Annemarie," I say.

"Thank you!" Annemarie practically sings.

Hazel reaches up and squeezes my shoulder. I think she's going to say something about Nightshade. I think that the excitement about the movie must be building up in her, the bubbles in a shaken-up bottle of orange soda. I turn around. All of them are wearing Very Berry. "Notice anything different about her?" she says. She nudges Annemarie and grins.

My excitement fizzles.

Annemarie kind of looks the same to me. I hope it's not a trick question. "Um, her scarf." It's plaid and I think I saw Lucy wearing the same one a week before.

Annemarie shakes her head and pulls back her hair in this exaggerated way. It must be a clue, so I say, "Your headband."

"No!" Hazel cries. "Her ears. They're double pierced now!"

I see it now. Two earrings instead of one. "Totally cute," I say. Annemarie smiles and I know I've said the right thing.

"Early birthday present. Don't tell her father." Annemarie's mother says it like there's a wink in her voice.

"Dad's going to flip," Annemarie says. "But it's worth it. Gina got me these earrings." She wiggled the lobes. They were little gold anchors. "And Lucy got me this nail polish." Annemarie's nails were painted a dark shade, almost black. "It's called Passionate Purple."

The girls in the back break into laughter and I'm not sure I get the joke.

"My gift's in my bag," I say. I looked through three issues

of *Teen Scene* to find the *right* thing. I knew it right when I saw it—this cool makeup bag with lipstick kisses all over it in different colors. Mom took me to the mall to buy it. I wrapped it in my favorite polka-dotted paper. "I didn't know it was already present time."

"It's just something we did before," Lucy says.

We. A pronoun for a group of people. A group that doesn't include me.

"They'll be plenty of time after the movie," Annemarie's mom says. Her words are soft and understanding. My ears burn because I know that tone. She feels bad for me.

"No big deal," Hazel says.

I force a smile. "No big deal."

Annemarie's mom drops us off at the door of the theater. "I'll be back in two and a half hours," she says. "Have fun!" Hazel and Lucy and Annemarie tumble out the back—all skinny jeans and fuzzy boots and laughter.

The excitement bubbles back up in me, too. The next Nightshade movie! I mean, I already know what happens, but seeing it up on the screen in the darkened theater, it's magical. The reflection of light off Nightshade's magnifying glass. The spark and flash of the wizard's wand. The fog and gloom of the magician's moat in the middle of the forest. It's all big and blown up. Larger than life.

It's almost like, for a moment, you're there. You're part of it. The real world falls away.

Annemarie pulls out the tickets from her purse and hands each of us one. "Mom gave me money for us to buy some snacks, too," she says. She holds up a twenty-dollar bill. "Anyone want something?"

I don't want to seem greedy, but Hazel and Lucy are only looking at each other. Annemarie shrugs and starts to put the bill away. "Red Vines?" I don't mean for it to be a question but it still comes out that way.

"Yeah—" Hazel starts, but suddenly her hand shoots out and grabs Lucy's arm. "Joey. Peters. Is. Here." She's saying this through gritted teeth and her face has turned as red as the cherry Icees churning behind the snack counter.

I turn to look.

"Don't look!" Lucy screeches. I flip back, confused. "We have to play it cool." She pretends to be looking at the ground, but her eyes sneak up every few seconds or so. "He's with Lamar Anthony and Evan Tibbs. He's wearing his blue jacket. His hair is swooped to the left."

"What do I do?" Hazel asks. She's biting her lip and some of the Very Berry has rubbed off on her teeth. I can't tell her, though, because Lucy's pushing her toward the arcade where the boys are playing Pac-Man on one of the old machines.

"We'll go and pretend we're interested in another game,"

she says. "They'll notice us and come over." This sounds like it's right out of a *Teen Scene* advice column.

"Why don't you just say hello?" I ask. I'm looking at my watch and we have only fifteen minutes before the movie starts. I don't want to miss a single moment of it.

"Are you kidding me? No. She can't do that," Lucy says. She rolls her eyes like it's totally obvious.

"We won't have time to get snacks."

Annemarie shoves the money my way. "Here. One thing of popcorn. No butter. And Red Vines."

I wait in line at the concession stand but turn around every few seconds or so to see what's going on in the arcade. I pretend I'm Nightshade, a detective. So far, here's what I see: Hazel, Annemarie, and Lucy are standing by the mechanical horse that you can ride for a quarter. The boys are super into their game. Their eyes don't leave the screen and they cheer every so often and slap each other on the back. There's the occasional high five. Annemarie and Lucy push Hazel closer. She swats at both of them but she doesn't seem unhappy about it. She's laughing. She doesn't try to move back.

I think I'm fine waiting here, looking on, but then there's this little sizzle of jealousy right under my skin. I don't like Joey Peters. But I do wonder how it would feel to be noticed.

"Next," a voice says. Then, in a little more of an annoyed

voice: "Next person in line!"

"Oh, that's me!" I say, reluctantly turning around.

I study the menu. "Red Vines, orange soda"—I grab a few straws out of the dispenser—"and a large popcorn."

I turn back around. The girl group and boy group have merged now—fused together like the slime mold Mrs. Judd showed us under the microscope in science class. Joey's shaking his swoopy hair out of his eyes. Hazel keeps touching his sleeve.

"With extra butter," I say. My own personal rebellion.

We're in our seats now. The movie theater darkens. A little hot dog with a top hat pops onto the screen, dancing and singing about the concession stand. Lucy leans over me to whisper something into Hazel's ear. She bumps the popcorn. A few kernels fall out into my lap.

She leans back in time for me to see the gigantic *No Talking in the Theater* reminder that both of them just broke. Then she taps me on the shoulder. "Hey, switch places, okay?" But Lucy doesn't wait for an answer and I'm standing, trying to juggle popcorn and Red Vines and napkins and my coat somehow. A mom a few rows down gives us a look.

Lucy slips into the chair I was in and now I'm on the outside again.

We're halfway into the movie when Lucy stands up. She's trying to hold giggles in, but they keep escaping like air out of a balloon. She crawls over my knees into the aisleway. "Bathroom," she explains. She looks back at Hazel and Annemarie.

Two minutes later, Annemarie is next. She's laughing and tripping over my sneakers and making a complete racket. She's not even trying to be quiet, and I can feel my face twisting up grumpy because this is the part where Nightshade and Starlight are sharing theories over cups of punch at Fizzy's. It's a small part, but it's my very favorite and I'm missing it.

"Bathroom." The word explodes out of her mouth tangled up with a laugh.

Now it's just me and Hazel. I'm watching the movie and I'm also watching her out of the corner of my eye. She reaches over and grabs my hand. "Em," she whispers. I turn.

Sometimes, when Mom drives me to Hazel's house at nighttime, she has to turn on the brights because Hazel lives out past the city where it's super dark. But the lights from the car illuminate everything around it.

That's Hazel right now. She's full-on bright in this theater. Lit up.

"We're going to sneak into *Fast Cars, Fast Times*," she whispers.

I've seen the previews for that. A bunch of people driving fancy cars like Ferraris and Lamborghinis at dangerous speeds and ladies wearing small swimsuits even though they're not at the beach.

"Why?"

She shrugs but her cheeks turn red. She grabs her lip gloss out of her pocket and smears some on her lips.

"It's Joey," I say. My words sound like an accusation.

"Come with us." She's squeezing my hand now. Smiling. Standing.

"But this is our thing," I say. "Nightshade and Starlight." I try to pull her back down to her seat, but she doesn't budge. "We love this. We've waited forever." My calendar says *Nightshade movie* in neon-pink highlighter. We counted down for the Nightshade movie. A plan *we* made. We. Me and Hazel and no one else. This was ours.

She shrugs again. I'm starting to hate that small little motion.

"Hazel, don't go. You'll get caught," I try. "You'll get in trouble. What about Dreamy Drew?" He's on the screen now and she's not even watching.

Now I'm the one holding on. She shakes my hand to let go.

"Stay," I plead. Maybe that one word will be enough.

She turns to leave.

"Starlight—"

"We're done with that," she says. Her words spark now. Tiny explosions. She doesn't turn around. "Don't be such a baby."

I grip the armrests so hard my knuckles turn white. I have to hold on to something.

She walks down the steps, turns the corner, and disappears out of sight.

I watch the rest of the movie through blurry eyes.

THE GREAT DIVIDE

I exit the movie theater alone.

I squint. The light out in the hallway is so bright compared to the theater. My head's pounding now, and even though my stomach sloshes with orange soda, I feel so empty. Like my insides have been scooped all the way out.

Fast Cars, Fast Times doesn't end for another twenty minutes. I can hear the car crashes and the explosions and music thumping even from out here. I throw away most of the popcorn, the remaining bit of soda, and three unopened straws.

I *actually* do have to go to the bathroom.

There's one at the very end of the hallway and when the door closes, it's totally quiet in there except for the fan above and this mister thing that sprays some floral scent. It's nice. Peaceful.

I lean over the sink and look at myself in the mirror. My eyes are rimmed red and puffy. Hazel would tell me to use cucumber slices or suggest some mask recipe from *Teen Scene*.

Hazel.

I pump the paper towel dispenser and run a piece under cold water. I hold it over my eyes and hope the redness goes away. I let myself into a stall. I hang my bag on the hook and I just sit there a minute. It's probably gross. There are probably a million germs on the tile floor and the walls and on the toilet itself, but I lean my head against the wall.

There's a movie in my mind. A horror movie. Hazel standing. Hazel pulling her hand away. Hazel calling me a baby. Saying we're done with the Unicorn Chronicles and her being Starlight and everything.

If that's all done, what do we have left?

The door to the bathroom opens. Three voices. I pull my knees up to my chest so that my feet don't show underneath the stall door.

"Joey so likes you," Lucy says. I picture her leaning over the sink and applying more lip gloss.

"I don't think so," Hazel says, but in this teasing voice that really means, *Yes I do.*

"Did you kiss him?" Annemarie asks.

"Guys, no," she replies. Another stall door opens. She's right next to me. "You were both there. Did you see him kiss me?"

"I bet he thought about it," Lucy says.

"Do you want to?" Annemarie asks. A sink starts. A toilet flushes.

"I don't know." She's quiet a moment. "Maybe," she says in a small voice.

Maybe! Maybe? That's a best friend kind of secret and she's never shared it with me.

One time Mina and I had been home alone and there was this totally terrifying movie on TV about duplicate pod people who take the place of the actual people living in the town. I had to sleep with my light on for days.

But that's what this is, I think. Some pod person Hazel, with highlights and field hockey friends and a heart for Jerky Joey, has taken over the body of best friend Hazel. It's the only thing that makes sense.

"I bet he'll be at the field hockey party." Annemarie dangles the information in the air.

"What? At Becca's?" Hazel's voice is a little breathy. Nervous. I picture her turning red. That's what happens to her—her arms, her face, her hands. A bright red Popsicle. Hazel hates when it happens.

"You could kiss him then."

"What? How? What about Becca's parents?"

"Upstairs." All three of them burst into giggles. A faucet turns on, then off.

"Where's Em?" Lucy asks.

"Still in the movie, I think," Hazel says. Her voice is neutral again. "Guys, I do feel kind of bad."

"She didn't want to go with you," Annemarie says matter-of-factly. "You said you asked her to come, which was way more than I would have done. You tried."

Hazel sighs. "You're right."

I want to scream right now. About the movie, about Hazel's secrets. I want to burst out of the stall and say, *You did not try. I tried. I've been trying.*

"How are you guys friends anyway?" Lucy asks. "She's like obsessed with those unicorn stories. I mean, they're *fine*, but she's like obsessed about them."

"Scary obsessed," Annemarie adds.

"Yeah," Hazel says slowly. "I guess it *is* a little much." A little much? She loves Nightshade just as much as I do. My stomach gurgles. I'm starting to feel sick.

"And what's with her and Hector?"

"They're both such weirdos," Annemarie says. She and

Lucy both crack up like she's said the funniest thing.

"Ms. Arnold's project," Hazel says, trying to explain maybe. Then I hate myself for thinking that. That she'd need to explain away Hector. "They were paired up."

"Soap Boy and the Letter M," Lucy says snottily. "How perfect."

I'm suddenly fiercely protective of Anita's nickname for me. It was mine and now it's wide out in the open for anyone to use. Lucy's twisted it and made it into something ugly.

I hear the pump of the paper towel dispenser and then the door opens and closes again. The voices disappear. My legs are limp from being in this weird crouching position, but the rest of me is on fire. I try to think about what Dr. Franklinton-Morehouse would tell me to do, but my brain's not even functioning now. My thoughts are coming out in long ribbon strands. They're twisting and knotting together in a way I don't understand.

It's all too much right now. There are so many bad feelings that have built up inside me that there's no more room.

I burst out of the door back into the hallway. Then I see her.

Hazel's in the lobby. She's laughing with Lucy and Annemarie. She doesn't see me approach, so she startles when I grab her sleeve. I hold it in my fist. "I need to talk to you," I say through gritted teeth.

The laughter stops. "Um, okay." She kind of gives the other girls this pinched-up face like she can't even believe I'm doing this. I pull her over to the arcade.

"I heard you in the bathroom," I say, pointing my finger at her chest. It sinks into her fuzzy scarf. My whole body feels uncomfortable right now, like I'm wearing the world's itchiest sweater. I hate how fuzzy her scarf is and how her hair's in this perfect ponytail and how her boots are actual Uggs instead of the knock-off ones Grandma got me from Target.

Hazel steps back like there's electricity running through my body and I've zapped her. "What? How?"

"I was in the stall."

"Spying on us?" she says. Her hands are on her hips now. I shrink.

No. No. I force myself to stand up straighter.

"I wasn't spying. It's a bathroom. I had to go." My voice is flat. "How could you let them say that stuff about me?"

"Em." Hazel's using her soft voice now. "Come on. They didn't mean it. They didn't know you were listening." Those two things are not the same. "Don't be so weird about it." But her eyes stray over to Lucy and Annemarie, who are watching us. It's clear to me now. Hazel's not really caring about me or what's happening in this moment or how very small I felt back in the theater. How very small I feel right now. She just wants to get back to them.

"No." I yank my hand away. My words are sharp. Pointy. "*You're* weird." They're the wrong words. They're Hazel's words. I can't seem to find my own.

I've never talked to Hazel this way. Not even when Hazel and I both wanted to be mermaid number two in Miss Murphy's Dance Academy show. Not even when we argued over what color M&M's to be for Halloween. Never. Ever ever. "All you care about is Joey and Lucy and field hockey and your stupid Very Berry lip gloss. I hate it."

There's a flash of something on Hazel's face at first. Surprise maybe. Her mouth forms a small O. Then her eyes narrow in on me, just like the Wizard's do in book two when he's about to blast the gnomes to smithereens.

"The only reason you got invited"—she starts. Her voice is building now. Each word feels like its very own exclamation point—"was because Gina couldn't come."

I squeeze my eyes shut. I'm far, far away now and back in time millions of years ago. This is how it must feel, I think. The shifts are small at first. You don't even know it is happening because all of it is occurring under the surface. Then, little by little, the divide gets bigger and bigger till one day, you look across the wide open ocean at the little speck of land in the distance and say how did that happen, even though it was happening the whole time.

How did this happen?

Millions of years of gigantic shifting plates or tiny moments across a few weeks.

I open my eyes. I'm not on the shores of Africa. I'm in Movie Time 8 and Hazel has her hands crossed over her chest and I have the uneaten Red Vines that we were supposed to share sticking out of the pocket of Mina's old coat. I focus on the little diamond pattern on the floor, the sound of the popcorn machine, the smell of nachos. I focus on anything but the look on Hazel's face and on the girls who are Hazel's friends, not mine, who I can feel watching from the concession stand.

"I was so right." Her eyes narrow. "You are a baby."

My mouth quivers. I can't hold it in anymore. Giant tears begin to plop on my sneakers. Slow at first and then faster and faster. I can't stop them. I wipe at my nose with my sleeve. Just like Lloyd Anderson.

Hazel didn't say anything because she agrees with them.

Finally, I find my voice. "Tell Annemarie's mom I got sick. Tell her my mom came to pick me up."

"What about your stuff?" Hazel asks coldly.

All I can do is stare at her boots. I can't even think about that right now. I just want Hazel to leave and everyone else to leave and to be left alone. "My mom will get it later." I'm doing this weird hiccup-y cry right now so the words barely get out.

Hazel says, "Okay." She hears me. She understands but she doesn't. Maybe that's it. Maybe there was a point when Hazel really stopped listening.

WAFFLE EMERGENCY

I grab more toilet paper from the bathroom.

There's a woman in there with two kids smaller than me. Both of them turn to stare. "Are you all right, honey?" she asks. She has a really kind mom voice—low and soft. It makes me want my own mom here so much.

"Everything's fine," I say. It just slips out, even though it's so clear from my snotty sleeves and bright red face that everything's not. I'm so in the habit of saying it.

I wait in there till I'm certain that Annemarie's mom has come and gone. Then I sit in the theater lobby on a bright red bench underneath some glowing sign for a movie called *Happy Dance!* Hippos with black-and-white canes and tilted top hats wear giant grins. It feels especially insulting right now.

I pull my cell phone out from my pocket, thankful that it's not in my overnight bag. I call Mom first, hoping that she's on some kind of break or something and can answer the phone. It goes to voicemail.

"Mom, it's me," I say. I struggle to keep my voice steady. "I'm not feeling good and I need to come home. Can you come get me?" I press the end call button and sigh, leaning my head against the wall. It could be a while.

And now I'm really not feeling well. I can't stay here.

I scroll down my contacts list and my thumb seems to stop on Mina's name automatically. I hesitate and think of the terrible words I said in her room that one morning. How I wasn't going to ask her for anything again. How I didn't need her. I close my eyes. I need her so much right now. I take a deep breath, and press call.

The phone rings once, twice and I'm thinking that this is a bad idea, the world's dumbest idea when she picks up.

"Hello?" she says. "Em?"

There's someone laughing in the background. Phoebe, I think.

"Mina," I say in this very small voice that I'm not sure she's even going to hear. "Mina."

"Yeah, Em." Mina's voice lowers. "Is everything okay?"

She shushes the person in the background. "What's wrong? I thought you were at the movies?"

"I was." I sniffle. "I mean, I am still. But Hazel—" I try again. "Hazel—they left me. I'm here alone." I'm doing the shuddering cry again and running out of dry toilet paper. "I need you."

"Oh God, Em." Mina whispers to someone in the background. "Okay, okay. Me and Phoebs are going to come get you. I just need to rinse this hair dye out."

"What?"

"But it won't take long. Just don't leave. Wait inside, okay? And don't talk to any strangers—even if they offer you candy or puppies or whatever."

I let out a laugh. It's short and quick but it does make me feel a little better. "I know that."

"Yeah, I know," Mina says. "But it made you laugh, right?"

Mina and Phoebe arrive twenty minutes later.

Mina texts me: We're out front. We've got puppies. JK.

They're in Phoebe's car, which is really Phoebe in car form. It's this old yellow Bug with Christmas plaid seats and a bunch of bumper stickers that say things like *Earth without Art is just Eh . . .* and *My child is an honor student at Rings Road Elementary School*, which she bought off the discount table at some thrift store for a quarter.

I have to stop myself from running to it: this little bit of sunshine in the middle of such a gray day.

Mina jumps out and puts the seat down so I can crawl into the back. She wraps her arms around me first. She's steady. Solid. We're the same height now, and it feels so good to let my head sink into her shoulder.

Mina pulls back and looks at me. "Whatever happened, Em. It's going to be okay."

Tears start running down my face again. "Okay, okay." Then I see it. What she was talking about on the phone. There's a bright pink stripe woven through the blond. I reach up to touch it. Her hair's still damp.

"Just like Nightshade's."

"Ha—you're right. I didn't even think about that. You like it?"

"Yeah." It makes her outsides look braver and bolder somehow.

"It felt like the right thing to do, you know?"

I climb in. The heater's going full blast, and there's a box of tissues waiting for me in the back. Phoebe turns around as Mina closes the passenger-side door. "What's going on?"

I want to tell them. But the problems seem so big right now and all I can picture in my brain is Hazel staring me down and calling me a baby. "Hazel—" I start. "She called me—" I try again. "And Gina couldn't come—" I can't get the words out. I blow my nose into the tissue and stuff it into my pocket.

Phoebe gives Mina a nod. "Waffles."

"Waffles?" I ask, but it kind of comes out like a wail.

"Waffles," Mina says.

I take in a deep breath and reach over the seat to squeeze Mina's shoulder. "I mean, is that okay?" I ask.

She turns back and gives me the smallest smile. "Yeah. It's okay."

Phoebe turns into a tiny parking lot at the very edge of town. It's almost completely full even though it's almost three p.m. and way past breakfast time.

Straight ahead is a building that looks like an old-fashioned train car. On the top of it, a glowing blue sign reads *EMERGENCY WAFFLES* in thick block letters. Standing on top of the sign is a waffle complete with a superhero cape. An oasis in the middle of Ohio.

"Ahh, do you smell that?" Phoebe says, locking the car.

"Bacon?" I ask.

"It's the smell of all our problems going away." She puts her arm around me and squeezes tight.

The diner is small. We grab a booth along the windows, Mina and Phoebe sliding into one side and me into the other. A waitress comes over with menus. She's wearing a cape, too, just like the Super Waffle on the top of the building. It's nice to feel rescued every once in a while, I think.

She fills Mina's and Phoebe's mugs with coffee. I turn mine upside down. I order a large orange juice instead and open up the menu. "Everything's waffles," I say, scanning down the choices. I squint a little. My eyes still ache from all the crying.

"Amazing, right?" Phoebe says. "It's like they've made the restaurant of my heart. I normally go with the Peanut Butter Surprise waffle."

"What's the surprise?" I ask.

"And spoil it for you?" Phoebe leans closer and fake whispers. "It's M&M's."

I take sneaky glances at Mina over the top of my menu. She puts hers down and picks it back up, but like it takes real effort.

So much of this is like our last visit to China Bistro. The smooth vinyl of the booths, the hum of people in the background, the clatter and clank of dishes and glasses bumping into each other. All of the good food smells are mixed together.

I suddenly get it, as if it's been written on the fogged-over window of the diner and suddenly made clear. It was hard for me. But it was also really, really hard for Mina. I didn't ask for this, but neither did she.

When the waitress comes back and flips her notepad to a new page, I half expect Mina to push away the menu and say she's not hungry. Instead, she takes a shaky breath and orders a waffle with fresh strawberries. Phoebs orders chocolate chip and I order the Peanut Butter Surprise, even though the surprise has been ruined.

"So what happened?" Mina asks. I don't like coffee but I just want to smell it. I wrap my hands around her mug and lift it to my nose.

I tell them. I start at the beginning. Or what I think is the beginning—it's hard to be sure. I tell them about the bookstore and Hector and the Slice. I tell them about Annemarie and Gina and Lucy with their perfect flat hair and arm bangles. I tell them about the new poster in Hazel's room, outdoor lunch, the invitation. I tell them about the movie. About what Hazel said.

At some point during the story, the waffles arrive, appearing on the table like plate-sized miracles.

"Okay, first of all," Mina starts, after I've said everything. She's waving her fork around like some crazed musical conductor. "Anyone can like the Unicorn Chronicles. Adults like the Unicorn Chronicles. There are *collector editions*. That are *expensive*. Besides—me and Phoebs like it. Are we babies?" Little drops of strawberry syrup polka-dot the table.

"Of course not," Phoebe says. "We are *extremely* mature

high school juniors. But that's not the real issue here. Real talk. Are you ready for this?"

I nod and brace my hands against the Formica table in preparation.

"Middle school blows."

Mina lets out this snort and slaps Phoebe on the arm at the same time. "Phoebs! Not helpful."

"What? Do you not agree? Okay, fine. Middle school is a lot like *The Hunger Games*." She must see the look on Mina's and my face, because she puts her hand up like she's stopping traffic. "Hear me out, okay? The arena—that's like school. And it's full of kids doing terrible things to other kids. I mean, there's not tracker jackers or whatever, but there's gym class. Or that horrible haircut I got the day before eighth-grade pictures. Or cafeteria meatloaf, and you're never really sure who to make an alliance with or who's going to stab you in the back. Okay—this is actually really brilliant." She turns to Mina. "Could I do this as a paper for Mr. Renz?"

Mina shakes her head, hiding a smile. The pink in her hair shimmers. "He'd hate it."

Phoebe gives a deep sigh. "I know. Because it's not the *Iliad* or Tolstoy or something by some dead white man. But anyway—you get out of middle school alive, you're doing great."

"How do I do that?"

"I'd say I volunteer as tribute for you, but I don't, I really don't. Been there, done that once. Never again. I don't know. Mina? Words of advice?" Phoebe stuffs a huge bite of waffle into her mouth. "I'm eating here."

Mina stares down into her cup of coffee and then looks up. "Middle school can be the worst. But it's not all bad. I met Phoebe there—"

"Excellent move."

Mina rolls her eyes. "And I joined choir and figured out that I really love history. Bad stuff happens. Like the gym incident—"

"The gym incident?" I ask.

"Oh, that was *awful*," Phoebe says. Mina glares at her and Phoebe stuffs in another huge bite and points to her mouth. "Eating!"

"But everyone's having a hard time. Everyone."

"Not Hazel," I say.

"Even Hazel," she says. "Nobody gets out unscathed. I'd say that you learn from it, and maybe you do. But sometimes bad stuff happens and someone who was your friend isn't your friend anymore or the gym incident happens. And it just stinks."

"Middle school stinks," Phoebe says. "I'll raise my glass to that." She lifts her mug in the air.

"Hear, hear," Mina says. She raises her mug into the air

and I raise my orange juice glass and we clink them together in the middle.

We're sitting in Phoebe's driveway in Mina's car, waiting for it to warm up, when Mina's phone rings.

Mina turns down the radio and picks up her cell phone. "Hi, Mom."

Oh no. My stomach sinks. I completely forgot I called her first. I take my own phone out of my pocket. Four missed calls.

"No, she's right here," Mina says.

"Tell Mom I'm sorry," I say, the words tumbling over each other. "I must have put it on silent or something." I picture Mom trying to call me again and again and me not answering. I hate that I made Mom worry more.

"She turned her phone off," Mina says. "It was an accident. Yeah. No. It was a friend thing. I'll tell her." She turns to me. "Mom was about to come looking for you."

Mina puts her mittened hand on mine. "She's okay. We're okay. We're together." She takes a deep breath. "Mom, today was a really good day." You know what? Even with what happened at the movies with Hazel, it really was. And if there could be one good day, I have to have hope that there could be more.

Maybe one day, the good ones will outnumber the bad.

Mina ends the call and puts the phone back into her bag.

"Thanks for coming," I say. The heater's warmed up the car now and I feel so cozy and exhausted but also happy.

"Thanks for needing me," Mina says. Then she plugs in her phone, chooses a song, and we sing at the top of our lungs. It feels great—like I'm letting something go.

Maybe this is a thing to know about growing up: There are some things in life you've got to hold on to. And there are other things you've got to let go.

The key is knowing the difference.

I don't let go of Mina's hand the entire way home.

MONDAY

Mina and Phoebe drive over to Annemarie's to pick up my stuff.

Hazel doesn't text me the rest of the weekend. I don't know what I expected—her to text me and tell me she's sorry? That she's made a mistake? She doesn't. And I don't either. Even though Dr. Franklinton-Morehouse says to forgive, I'm not feeling ready. Everything still feels too fresh.

So on Sunday, I'm feeling pretty mopey. I finally get tired of lying in my bed, so I get up and lie on the floor instead. I slip my earbuds in and press play on the next CD.

"Hello, my friends," he says. His voice is so calm and soothing. It kind of makes me want to fall asleep again. "It's me again. Dr. Franklinton-Morehouse. But you knew that." He chuckles. "We have a final step to talk about today. It's another tool to add to your *Be the Best You* toolbox. What I'm talking about today is listening. Listening is one of the most important skills you can develop.

"Listening builds so many things. It builds compassion. It builds empathy. It builds understanding. Listening to others shows that we care. Not only that, though, listening to others allows us to reflect on who we are personally. When we let someone else's experiences in, we grow in so many different ways. That, too, shapes us.

"I want you to listen. To me. To people around you. Also, listen to yourself. You have a voice inside your head. Too often, we ignore it. You often know the right thing to do."

I sit up straight. I know what I need to do. It's what I should have done the very first week of school.

On Monday morning, I have Mom drop me off early. I walk into school and straight to Ms. Arnold's room. I don't even stop at my locker.

The door is open just a smidge and there's a new *Bagel Bunch* sign on the door. This bagel has an eye patch and looks like a pirate. I hear laughing and cheering and someone shouts. Lloyd maybe. "Got you again," he says.

I take a deep breath and knock.

A second passes. Hector appears at the door. He pokes his face out and grins like it's totally normal and he expected to see me there. "What's the secret password?"

"Um, *bagel bunch*?"

"Ugh, Emily. Are we so uncreative? No. Try again."

"Hector, let her in," I hear Anita yell in the background.

"Fine, fine." He shakes his head. "The secret password was *asparagus*."

"How was I supposed to get that?"

"You weren't. It's secret."

Hector opens the door and I walk in and suddenly I feel a little shy, like here I am, busting in on their Bagel Bunch meeting when they were probably happy with the original members.

Ms. Arnold rises from her desk. She was grading papers. "Em, we're so glad you're here." She hands me a box and a napkin. "Doughnut hole?"

"We're equal-opportunity breakfast," Sara says.

"But we can't change the name of the club," Hector says. "We shall forever be the Bagel Bunch, no matter what we eat."

"I was wondering," I say. I take a deep breath. "I was wondering if maybe I could join."

"Our game?" asks Lloyd. They've pushed all the desks together in a big rectangle. There are markers in the center.

"No, well, yes," I say. "I'd like to play. But I mean the Bagel Bunch."

"You have to put a bagel on your head and swear a solemn oath," Hector says, holding his hand up like he's about to recite a pledge.

"Really?" It sounds strange but I'm willing to do it.

"No," Anita says. "You're already a part of the group, Em."

I let her words sink in.

Hector and the Unicorn Chronicles and his figurines. Anita and her dancing and dreams of space. Sara and her cat clothes. Lloyd and survival and that strange but really addicting show.

And me, self-help-CD-listening, unicorn-loving, not-at-all-perfect Emily.

As great as it would be to make the Junior Roosevelts, I already feel like I've made one team. I belong. I've belonged all this time.

"Ready to play?" Lloyd says.

I count the markers on the table. "There aren't enough."

"That's on purpose," Sara says. "It's part of the game. Normally you play with spoons, but Ms. Arnold wouldn't let us grab some from the cafeteria."

"I said to be resourceful," Ms. Arnold chimes in. She's grinning at me. "It's a life skill."

"Anyway," Anita says. "If there are seven players, you

put six markers in the center. Everyone starts off with four cards. Only you can see your cards. The dealer starts passing cards around the circle. You can keep your card or pass."

"But you can only have four cards in your hand at a time," Hector says. "You're trying to get four of a kind. Like four kings or four fives. Once you do, you grab a marker real sneaky-like."

"Like this," Sara says. She takes a marker from the center like a unicorn spy.

"And then," Lloyd says, "once someone notices, everyone tries to take a marker." He grabs one. Then the rest of them lunge. Only I'm left without one. "It's like *Island Adventure: Uncensored, Classroom Edition.*"

"Except not at all." Sara laughs.

"It gets vicious," Ms. Arnold says. "I'm on the injured list right now."

"See!" Lloyd says. He nudges Sara's shoulder. "Exactly the same."

Hector's face grows red. "Sorry about that again."

Ms. Arnold laughs. "It's fine. But fair warning, okay." She winks at me.

It takes me one or two times playing, but I finally get the hang of it. On the third time, I raise the yellow marker in the air triumphantly.

"One of us," Hector says, like he's an alien. The rest of

them join in. "One of us."

My heart feels so big, like it's going to burst.

It turns out that I'm not quite as bad at the Circle Break game as I thought. Maybe the key is finding people who actually want to let you in.

ALL THE LITTLE PIECES

On the first day of Thanksgiving break, we finish the puzzle.

"You put in the last piece," Mina says to me. She's still in her duck slippers and robe.

"No," I say. "We have to do it together." It feels like such a moment. I hold the piece up in the air. Mom and Mina and I each take a corner. "Okay, on the count of three."

"One, two, three!" Mina cheers. We snap the piece into place and all applaud.

Bean looks proud from her place on the floor, like we're clapping for her. "Okay, now what?" Mom asks.

I get an idea. "Hold on, you and Mina stay here." I run into the kitchen and open the glasses cabinet next to the fridge. I stand on my tippy-toes and pull down three of the fancy goblets. I blow out the dust and rinse them off in the sink.

I open the fridge and move aside the cheeses, opened jars of spaghetti sauce, and the turkey we'll have for Thanksgiving dinner that's still a little bit frozen. I don't find any sparkling grape juice, so I pull out the next-best thing. I pour a little apple juice into each glass and carry them into the dining room.

"Time for a celebration!" I say.

Mom smiles at me with the same smile she did in the dressing room right before school started. Her *you're growing up* smile.

We each take a sip. It tastes better than I remembered.

Later, when Mina's doing stats homework at the library and Mom's baking a pumpkin pie, I go back into the dining room.

Pretty amazing! Five thousand pieces.

"I've got to show Hazel," I say to Bean and I take a picture with my phone.

Emily: Look! We're done!

Then I remember. I don't press send. It joins all the other unsent texts. I put my phone away. The bubbly feeling I had before fizzles a little.

Being best friends with Hazel is a hard habit to break.

SNOW DAY

Snow comes early to Ohio.

Normally, the first good snow comes in January. But here it is, end of November, and when I get up in the morning to let Bean out to go to the bathroom, I see the yard has been covered in a layer of thick white. I pull Bean's sweater out of the hall closet and slip it over her head, poking her two front legs through the open armholes. I yank on my hat and boots and zip up my winter coat right over my pajamas.

Bean and I tumble out the back door. It's quiet except for our breathing that comes out in frozen puffs like we're winter dragons and the crunch of our boots and feet. It's dark, too. The only light comes from the lamp suspended above the door.

There's this sensation you get when you're up before the rest of the world and you feel like it's your own. Possibility, maybe.

Bean finishes going to the bathroom and trots back to me with a little snow beard hanging off her chin. It makes her look especially distinguished, I think. The snow suits everyone.

Back inside, I shake off my boots and I turn on the news. The weather lady is cheerful because weather is happening. They cut to another person outside the school bus yard picking up snow with her gloved hand and measuring it with a ruler.

The main newscaster comes back on. She looks very warm and snug at her desk. "There are going to be a lot of happy kids waking up this morning," she says. "For the latest school delays and closings, check out the bottom of the screen."

A bright blue ribbon of text scrolls by, listing schools in alphabetical order. They're on the Ps, so I'll have to wait till they circle around again. But then my phone illuminates: a text from Hector.

Hector: Snow Daaaaaaaaaa
Hector: aaaaaaaaaaay!!!!

Hector: (Mom just got the call from school!)
Emily: Hooray!!
Hector: (you're a poet and didn't know it—ha ha)
Emily: Ha ha

I put my phone down on the couch and run into the kitchen. This is cause for celebration. I open the fridge. Mom's bought cinnamon rolls that come in one of those airtight cans. I heat up the oven to 350 and open the rolls with a satisfying *pop*.

I wait for the good cinnamon smells to wake Mom and Mina up: that's the best kind of alarm clock. Bean and I go into the dining room. We're starting a new puzzle. Mom bought it at the store, special. It's of a bunch of greyhounds wearing Santa hats.

Bean hears a rustling upstairs and runs out of the dining room to discover who's up. After a moment or two, Mom pokes her head in the door. Her hair's sticking up on one side. "Morning," she says. "You're up early."

"And I'm making breakfast," I say. "It's a snow day!"

Mom raises her hands in the air like she's a boxer. She cheers. "Whoo-hoo. That's exciting. I bet Mina's off, too."

She leaves and then I hear the sounds of the coffeemaker and mugs clanking together.

I hear the shuffle of Mina's slippers next.

She's got the robe I gave her last Christmas wrapped around her. It has tiny smiling donkeys on it. She sits down and takes a sip of my juice. "Phoebs just texted me," she says. She looks out the window. The snow is still coming down in big, fat flakes. "I bet Dr. Oliver won't want me to come in today either." She sniffs the air. "Cinnamon rolls?"

I nod. Mina looks to Mom, her forehead crinkled. "I'd like to have one."

"Then I think you should," she replies. "We'll all eat together."

Mina relaxes at this. "But I'll still have to go into the bank," Mom says. She has her cup of coffee now. "Do you girls think you'll be able to handle things here okay?"

"I'm in high school. And Em's in sixth grade. Practically an adult."

Mom squeezes her arm. There's something to hold there now. "And I'm your mom. It's my job to worry."

"I know." Mina puts her arm around me. "You be careful, too," she says to Mom.

"We'll all just worry about each other," I say.

"Let's go sledding," Mina says all of a sudden, sometime in between *Good Morning America* and *The Price Is Right*. It's just like Mina to have a great idea at the right moment. More and more bits of the old Mina are shining through.

253

I look out the window. Large flakes have started to fall again. I remember the crunch of the snow beneath my boots from earlier. Thick, wet packing snow. The best kind for sledding.

"Why don't you text your friends?" she says, standing up and stretching out after being curled up on the couch all morning. "I'll call Phoebs. The roads shouldn't be so bad now. Darby Creek, you think?"

Dad used to take us to that park years ago—me and Mina and Hazel. It has the steepest, slipperiest sledding hill in Columbus and is only a little drive away. There's a little piece of me that's sad when I think about it. Sad that it's not going to be me and Hazel this time. But a bigger part of me is happy.

I text Hector and Anita: Sledding?

They respond at nearly the same time: YES!

I grin. I know just where the sled is. I run down the stairs into the basement and find it right next to Mom's think-about pile. I'm glad we didn't give it away. The silver runners still shine.

We pick up Phoebe first. She's wearing a beret. It's not the most practical choice, but it makes her look very French and very Phoebe. "I'm a Francophile now," she says dramatically when I ask her about it.

"Since when?"

Mina laughs. "Since we got a new exchange student in

school two weeks ago."

Phoebe shoves her arm. "Hey, I've always appreciated the French. Their cheese. Their bread. Their freestanding towers."

"And their boys . . ."

Phoebe turns around in her seat and waggles her eyebrows at me. "What's not to like, right? Phoebe and Jacques does have a very nice ring to it. Let's study abroad in college, Mina. Two girls, making their way through Paris."

"We could do that." I hear the smile in Mina's voice.

When we get to Hector and Anita's they must be waiting at the door, because they are already running out by the time Mina honks the horn. They smoosh into the backseat with me—Hector in the middle because he's the smallest. He doesn't complain.

"Mina Murphy!" Hector says, reaching into the front seat for a high five. "Girl I don't know!"

"That's Phoebs," I say. "Phoebe, this is Hector and Anita."

"Your hat is *awesome*!" Anita says.

"*Merci beaucoup*," Phoebe replies.

I whisper in an extra-loud voice so everyone can hear, "She's French now."

The hill is extra crowded today. It seems like everyone had the same idea as we did. There's something about a first snow that feels exactly like the first day of summer. Maybe it's the closest to magic we'll ever get.

In all the bustle, Mina still manages to find a place to park. We tumble out. We're marshmallows in our puffy coats and extra socks. Hector looks around wide-eyed. "Remember when Ice Apocalypto turned the entire unicorn underworld into his ice kingdom? This looks exactly like that."

It really does.

I pull our sled from the trunk and Anita grabs their circular flying saucer they brought along. "Race you to the top," she says, and she runs flying up the right-side hill, her braids bouncing behind her. Hector and I follow behind. The path has already been worn down by the feet of other sledders, but it's still a lot harder to run on snow.

We finally reach the top, breathless. The entire hill stretches out before us.

Anita bounces from one boot to the other. "I'll go first," she says. I laugh. I'm not surprised. Hector holds the back of the saucer for her as she positions her bottom in the middle. She grabs hold of the two side straps. "Gimme the biggest push."

"Ready," Hector says. I place my hands on Anita's back. "One, two, three!" We both dig our boots into the snow and heave.

Anita lets out a delighted scream and goes careening down the hill. Mina and Phoebe, who have almost made it to the top, stop and watch and wave as she goes flying by.

When she gets to the bottom, she leaps up and raises her arms into the air triumphantly. Hector and I clap.

"You up next?" Hector asks.

"Let's go together," I say. I climb onto the sled first. Hector slides in behind me and puts his hands around my waist. I grab onto the rope looped on the front to steer. We inch the sled closer to the drop-off with our feet. "Here we go!"

We start off slow. But then, suddenly, we start to pick up speed. "Wahoo!" I hear Hector call behind me. The wind whips in my face and through my hair. I'm grinning so hard that my cheeks hurt from the effort. I picture Nightshade running through the night with Starlight by her side. I bet that this is how she feels.

I pull up on the rope to slow us down near the bottom.

"That was awesome!" Hector says. "Awesome."

We take turns after that. Mina and Phoebe. Me and Anita. Hector takes a turn with everyone. On our final ride down, we hook the saucer to the back of the sled, and we all ride down together. I hold my hands up the entire time.

When we get back into the car, I catch a glimpse of myself in the rearview mirror. My eyes are red-rimmed from the cold and tears streak my windburned face. I have looked the same way so many times this year. But today, it's for the best of reasons.

LETTING GO

The house is drafty and dark when we get home.

We strip off our wet clothes at the door and change into our pajamas because it's that kind of day. Mom left a lunch plate for Mina in the fridge, everything pre-portioned out. I make a peanut butter and banana sandwich, and we sit together at the table.

Mina eats slow but she finishes everything.

"Want to build a fire?" Mina asks. It feels like the cold has soaked down into our bones.

"Do you know how?" I think of the stacks of split logs out back that have sat lonely since Dad left. We haven't had a fire in a long time.

"Sure," Mina says. "I saw Dad do it a bunch of times."

Bean and I settle into the family room while Mina grabs a few logs and smaller sticks from outside. She stacks them in the fireplace.

Then she sets balls of newsprint in between the logs. She rolls one of the pieces up like a hot dog and lights the end. She sticks it up into the chimney. "You have to make sure the flue is open," she says. "Or else all the smoke will come into the house."

Finally, she holds a match to the pyramid. The paper catches fire. Slowly, the flames spread to the logs. Soon, the fire crackles and pops.

Bean is stretched out in front of it. I snuggle deeper into my blanket.

We sit there for a while in the quiet. But it's not the alone kind of quiet I've felt before. Or the bad quiet where I'm just waiting for something to go wrong.

This is a good quiet where two sisters are just happy to be together.

"We'd had these big bonfires at Pinehurst," Mina says when the fire's died down a little.

I sit back. I listen.

"They'd have these little slips of paper for us to write on. We could put whatever was holding us back—feelings we were having or secrets. It feels good, you know.

You feel lighter somehow."

She pauses a moment, looks at me. "Does that sound ridiculous?"

"No." I shake my head. "No." I picture the tiny pieces of paper curling up in the heat. Turning into ash. Disappearing. "We could do that now," I say. I want to do that now.

"You think?" she says. "Maybe we should."

"I've got paper." I jump up and run for the stairs, my blanket trailing behind me. Up in my room, I grab a couple of index cards and my nicest pens from my top desk drawer. I'm quick. Just as I turn to leave, a flash of white catches my eye.

It's the definition of who I wanted to be. I read it again.

Em Murphy (noun)
Cool.
Girl who fits in.
Best friends with Hazel.
Friends with Lucy, Annemarie, and Gina.
Knows the right things to do (hair, boy stuff, clothes).
Fancy-pants.

I unpin the definition from my bulletin board and slip it underneath the stack of note cards.

I hand Mina a few of the cards when I'm back downstairs.

I sit back on the couch. What do I need to let go of?

On one card, I write *Dad and Alice.*

On another card, I write *Hazel.* Or maybe it's more *things staying the same.* I write that down, too.

Mina folds her papers into tiny little stars.

"All right," she says. "Whenever you're ready, you can let them go."

I hold the papers tightly in my fist. Dad and Alice and Hazel and things staying the same. I also hold the definition of Future Me. Or really, who I thought Future Me should be. Turns out they're not really the same thing at all.

I let go. I watch the papers fly from my fist and land in the flames. They glow orange and red and yellow. They twist and turn. They shrink down into nothing.

They disappear.

THINGS THAT SURPRISE YOU

It's the first Saturday night in December and there's a knock at the door.

At first I think I've imagined it. Bean and I are in my room. I'm piecing together a dinosaur costume for her and I've just texted Sara a picture of my progress. I have all my green fabric laid out in front of me, and I'm cutting the triangle teeth out of white felt. Mom's downstairs in the basement doing more organizing, and Mina's out with Phoebs and Jenna at the high school hockey game.

I hear it again. But it's not so much a knocking this time as it is a pounding.

"Mom, you hear that?" I call down.

Bean and I run down the stairs to the front door. I flip on the outside light and peek out the window. No one.

Pound, pound.

It's coming from the back door. Now I'm kind of concerned it's a robber or murderer or something, but I wonder if they would announce themselves in such a way. Still, I yell down the basement steps to be safe. "There's someone at the back door."

"What?" Mom yells.

Bean skids across the hardwood floor, running at full speed. I follow behind her. She stops at the door out to the backyard patio. She looks between me and the door, her body jiggling. Bean is not a very good watchdog.

I turn the lock and pull the door open and there's Hazel. My eyes go big. But it's not Best Friend Hazel or Highlights Hazel or Lunchtime Hazel who barely looks at me now from her table with the other field hockey girls. This Hazel's face is red and streaky. Her coat's half off her shoulder and not zipped, even though it's freezing. Her fuzzy boots, which look like all the other girls' fuzzy boots, are soaked through from the earlier snow.

Mom's joined me at the door and it's she who moves first. She gathers Hazel in and pulls her into the house all at the same time. I close the door but the chill doesn't leave the air.

"What's wrong?" Mom asks. She's holding Hazel at arm's length right now. "Are you all right? Does your mom know you're here?"

Hazel shakes her head and her shoulders heave. A snot bubble forms at her nose, and I run to grab a tissue for her from the bathroom. On second thought, I grab the whole box and hand it to her.

She starts to talk but I can barely make out any words because they're so shuddery. But I do make out the words *Becca* and *field hockey* and I put the puzzle pieces together in my mind. "Becca's party." The one I had heard about in the bathroom. "You were there."

Hazel nods. She blows her nose hard into the tissue. It sounds a little like a honking bird.

"Oh, honey," Mom says. She squeezes Hazel around her shoulders. She turns to me. "I'm going to call Hazel's mom to let her know she's at our house. Why don't you get her some dry clothes."

Hazel removes her boots and peels off her wet jacket and leaves them in a heap on the floor. Upstairs, she changes into one of my old T-shirts, a pair of sweatpants, and some fuzzy socks. We sit cross-legged on my rug. Bean lays her head on Hazel's knee because Bean always knows what to do. Dogs are always their best selves.

We just sit there for a while. Hazel's rubbing Bean's bald

spot. It's where she likes to be rubbed the best. Hazel knows that, of course.

I can hear the rise and fall of Mom's muffled voice on the phone downstairs in between Hazel's sniffles. I hand her another tissue. I have so many questions. Like: What happened? Like: Why come here? But I'm hearing Dr. Franklinton-Morehouse in my brain and he's telling me just to listen.

"Joey Peters tried to kiss me," she blurts at once. My mouth falls open wide like a gaping fish, and I don't shut it quick enough because Hazel's face twists again. Tears pool in her eyes. "I turned, though. He got my ear."

"What? Why?" I'm remembering back to her conversation in the movie theater bathroom. "I thought you wanted to kiss him," I whisper.

She starts wailing again. "Yes. Maybe. I thought I did. I don't know. We were in this circle and there were a bunch of kids—boys and girls. Eighth graders. Girls from the team. Joey spun the bottle and it landed on someone else, but then Lucy turned it so that it pointed to me. And no one said anything. Everyone was watching." She covers her face with her hands like she can't even bear remembering.

"How—how did it feel?" I don't think it's the right question, but it escapes my mouth before I can stop it.

She thinks for a minute. "Do you remember when we were in Girl Scouts?"

I nod.

"And we went to the aquarium in Kentucky. Remember that tide pool?"

The aquarium was what inspired some of our best car dancing moves. "Yeah."

"Did you feel the snail's body?" She peeks out at me through two fingers.

I suddenly get what she's saying. "Oh no!" I scream and then slap my hand over my mouth.

A laugh bursts out from Hazel and suddenly she can't stop.

"It was like the snail"—she takes a deep breath—"was on my face!"

Hazel and I are on our backs now and I can hardly breathe I'm laughing so hard. It's just like how it used to be when we'd sit together in her room and watch YouTube videos of kids coming home from the dentist or this strange fox dance or a Jell-O mold that won't stop shaking.

Hazel and I are both quiet. She's still looking up at the ceiling when she says, "They laughed at me. And Joey. But mostly me." She sniffles.

Her next words are whispered. I have to scoot closer to hear. "Lucy called me a baby." She pauses and won't turn to meet my eyes. "In front of everyone."

There are so many things I could say right now.

I want to say something smart. Or something that will make her feel like the almost kiss and the laughter and the snow-soaked boots never happened. Or maybe that I know how being called a baby feels. But I can't think of anything right, so I reach over and take her hand and squeeze it.

When Hazel's mom arrives to pick her up, we're eating Double Stuf Oreos Mom's pulled out of the pantry. Mom calls it a feel-better food. I believe her. Hazel holds one out to me. "Go ahead and twist," she says. "We'll split it."

Part of me really wants to, but I shake my head. "That's okay. I'll have my own."

Once Hazel leaves, Mom sits back down at the kitchen table with me. She grabs an Oreo from the package and dunks it into my glass of milk. She points it at me. "When did you get to be so smart?"

I was feeling pretty good until this moment, but now the Oreos and milk are sloshing around together in my stomach. I scrape at the icing with my fingernail. I concentrate on the table. "I have something to tell you," I say.

Now I peek up, just a little. Mom's forehead lines fold into deep creases.

I take a deep breath. "Back in September, I kind of did

something bad. I ordered these CDs." My words crash together like bumper cars, like if I don't get the words out fast enough the story will stay inside me forever. "I couldn't sleep and there was this infomercial that told me I could be a better me and I thought that sounded pretty good because I felt so bad about things with Mina and things were going wrong with Hazel. I thought this would fix everything. But I didn't have enough money." I add the last part really quietly. "I used your credit card. I'm sorry."

Mom opens the drawer where she keeps all the bills. "September, you say."

I nod glumly.

She riffles through the papers. She pulls one out and unfolds it.

"They're *Be the Best You* CDs," I say. She scans the paper. "Or Mind over Matter Industries maybe."

Mom's trying to keep a straight face but a little grin peeks through. Then a giggle escapes from her lips. Then a bigger one. Soon she's laughing as hard as Hazel and I laughed in my room. "Oh, Em," she says. "Oh, Em."

She takes a tissue from the box sitting on the table and dries her eyes.

"After the year we've had—" Mom takes my hand in hers. "It's okay. I thought you were going to tell me something terrible."

"This isn't terrible?"

"No, no. I mean, you shouldn't have used my credit card."

"I know." My voice trembles. "I'm awful. I know it's yours and only supposed to be for emergencies. But to be honest, this really felt like an emergency."

"I actually saw this before," Mom says. "But I just thought it was another charge from Mina's stay at Pinehurst. There were so many of them, I didn't even think about it. But honey, why didn't you tell me all this? About everything with school and Hazel?"

"I don't know," I say. It's hard for me to find the words. "My problems seemed so small. You had bigger stuff to worry about. And you always look so tired and stressed out. I didn't want to add on my stuff to the pile."

Mom stands and holds out her arms. "Come here."

She wraps her arms around me and squeezes me tight. "I am tired and I am stressed, but you're my daughter. Just like Mina. Just as important as Mina. I'm sorry if I ever made it feel like you weren't. I care about you and your problems." She holds me out at arm's length. "Were the CDs any good?"

I laugh. It feels good. "Yeah. Dr. Franklinton-Morehouse knows his stuff. You could borrow them." I think about that for a moment. "I mean, you can have them. They're techni- cally yours, I think."

She strokes my hair like she did when I was eight. It's exactly what I need.

"You're a good mom," I say.

When she finally says something, her voice sounds heavy and thick. "I'm trying."

I really think that trying's the best that any of us can do.

CHANGE

Hector and I dress up for our presentation. He wears one of his dad's bow ties. I wear the same outfit I wore for school picture day. It makes me feel good.

Hector's mom drops him and Anita off at school because he's carrying our secret prop in a special cooler bag that you bring along to church potlucks.

"Are you ready?" he says. He's stopped at my locker. One of the older girls from the Roosevelts has taped an Eleanor on my locker. She's outlined in glitter. I still can't believe I made the team. We have our first competition in two weeks. Anita and Sara and I are riding together. I can't wait.

He shuffles through his index cards again and again.

"Ready for it to be done," I say. I couldn't even finish my cereal this morning.

Yesterday, Steve and Sara presented. They did the history of dance, complete with demonstrations from each era and costumes Sara had created. It was going to be hard to follow.

"I got you something, though." I pull the tissue-paper-wrapped package out of my backpack and hand it to him.

He unwraps it and holds the miniature dinosaur in his hand. "Whoa!" His eyebrows jump. "A Troodon. This is awesome!" His grin is huge. All teeth.

"From the gift shop."

"I'm going to keep it in my locker. A place of honor. A guard dinosaur." He holds his hand up. We high-five. No one messes with a Troodon pack.

Ms. Arnold claps her hand to get the class's attention. Hector and I have tacked up our poster to the cork strip and are standing at the front of the classroom.

"All right," she says. "Today we have Hector and Em."

"Just Emily," I whisper.

"Hector and Emily. They'll be presenting on the movement of the earth." Ms. Arnold walks to the back of the room with her clipboard and grade book. Hector clears his throat.

"A long time ago. Before you were born. Before your parents were born. Before the dinosaurs were born, the earth came to be. It's not the earth we recognize today. In fact, you couldn't have lived on earth. It was pretty much one big giant volcano. There was no crust, no place to stand, and it was hot," Hector begins. He looks at me. I nod.

"Even if there had been land, you wouldn't have been able to breathe. There wasn't enough oxygen. The air would have been poisonous to you."

I flip to my note card. "Over time, though, things changed. The earth cooled, which meant there was land to stand on. But it did not look like this classroom map now." I point to Ms. Arnold's rolled-down map. "Instead it looked like this." I point to the poster Hector and I created. "This landmass was called Pangaea."

"Over time, Pangaea split apart very, very slowly," Hector says. "This is because of the movement of the giant plates that make up the earth's surface. They float on magma like blown-up rafts on a pool. Their movement causes things to happen. Earthquakes rumble, volcanoes explode, land moves apart. Our earth is still changing. One day far in the future, the continents will form another big landmass."

"The earth is constantly moving," I say. "In space, it's spinning and revolving. The earth's plates are shifting and crashing and slipping. And we don't even know it. We can't feel that movement is happening until we look around and see day turn into night. Or winter turn into spring. Or there's an earthquake or volcano or the coast of Africa and the coast of South America no longer fit together like two snug puzzle pieces."

"There was this Greek guy, Heraclitus. He said the only thing constant is change. That was pretty smart, and it's true. So here's what we've got to do: keep our feet planted firmly on the ground and look around every once in a while. The world is so, SO much bigger than us."

I look up at Ms. Arnold. She's leaning forward in her desk and smiling.

"And," Hector says, "here's the best part. We've created a *very accurate* model"—he takes the foil off the metal tray and leans it up a little so the class can see—"of plate tectonics using pudding and candy bars. The pudding represents the magma and the candy bars represent the different plates. If you push them together, you can see how they sometimes slip underneath each other or could create new mountains. We also have spoons."

He holds one of the plastic spoons in the air. "Who's hungry?"

Everyone looks at Ms. Arnold for permission. When she nods, they jump out of their seats and gather around the tray. Hector passes out the spoons.

"That was awesome," Lloyd says, patting me on the back. He already has pudding on his sleeve. It's *so* Lloyd; now it just makes me smile.

"The awesomesauciest?" I ask.

Lloyd grins and bumps my fist with his. "Yeah, it was."

I step back next to Hector. "We did great," he says.

We did.

When the bell rings, the class clears out. Hector tells me he'll see me on Saturday. We're all going ice-skating at the Chiller—the whole Bagel Bunch. I've never been before, but Sara says I'll be a natural. "It's dancing, on ice, on teeny tiny blades," she says. "You'll be great."

I hang back.

"Great presentation, Emily," Ms. Arnold says. She's cleaning up the classroom. I help her take a bunch of the napkins to the trash can. "I would have never thought about pudding and candy bars for a model. But it's brilliant. And delicious." She pops the last mini candy bar into her mouth. "You and Hector make quite the team."

"Thanks," I say. I'm quiet for a moment. I bend one of the leftover plastic spoons in my hand. "Can I ask you question?"

"Sure." Ms. Arnold takes a seat on top of her teacher desk just like she did on the very first day of school. Today her shoes look like little New York taxicabs. There are so many things to like about Ms. Arnold.

"When you paired up me and Hector"—I start to ask— "Was that on purpose?"

"Here's what I'll say," she answers. "A lot of times, life works itself out. The people you meet, the friends you make, the things you do. But sometimes, I think, people need a little push in the right direction." She shrugs and smiles. "Does that answer your question?"

"Yeah," I say. "Yeah."

I'm about out the door when I turn back around again. "Hey, Ms. Arnold—"

She looks up from her papers.

"Remember that book you told me about? With the frizzy-haired girl on the front? Do you think maybe I could read it now?"

She opens her top desk drawer and pulls out the book. "It's been waiting for you."

I add it to the top of my stack of books. Anastasia stares back at me. "Thanks. And this is going to sound kind of random. But do you have a book about these kids who live in a museum? In New York?"

Ms. Arnold claps. "Yes! I know just the one." She walks over to the tall colorful bookcases that line the wall. She runs her finger along a middle shelf. "Here it is. *From the Mixed-Up Files of Mrs. Basil E. Frankweiler.* You'll love it. One of my favorites."

I'm reading before I'm even out the door. I start at the beginning.

AUTHOR'S NOTE

Things That Surprise You, in part, was inspired by my younger sister's years-long struggle with an eating disorder. While her own story is not mine to tell, I felt I could give voice to the guilt, sadness, and various difficulties families face when someone they love is struggling.

Eating disorders, like anorexia and bulimia, are serious and can be life threatening. If you or someone you know is struggling with disordered eating or experiencing the signs and symptoms of an eating disorder, I encourage you to reach out. Please talk to your parent or guardian, a trusted teacher, or a school counselor. They can direct you to the professional help and intervention you or your loved one needs. It can be scary, but it is so important that you not keep it to yourself. Know that you can get help. I've listed some general resources below.

The road to recovery can be long and difficult, but there is hope—for the individuals affected and for those who love them.

KidsHealth:
http://kidshealth.org/en/kids/eatdisorder.html#

National Association of Anorexia Nervosa and Associated Disorders:
www.anad.org

National Eating Disorders Association:
www.nationaleatingdisorders.org

National Institute of Mental Health:
www.nimh.nih.gov/index.shtml

ACKNOWLEDGMENTS

I think it will surprise no one that writing a book and sending it out into the world takes the work and support of a lot of wonderful people.

A big thank-you to my agent, Victoria Marini; to my editor, Alessandra Balzer, who helps me discover the magic in every story; to Kelsey Murphy and the rest of the awesome team at Balzer + Bray; and to Kathrin Honesta for illustrating one of the loveliest covers I've ever seen.

Thanks also go out to Corey Ann Haydu, Melissa Baumgart, the Grou, and all of my middle grade writer friends.

I'm so grateful, also, to the students and staff of St. Brigid of Kildare School. You welcomed me first as a teacher and then as an author. Thank you!

My appreciation also goes out to Dr. Kathryn Leugers who offered her professional opinion on this manuscript.

Any mistakes or inaccuracies are mine alone.

Thank you to Kurt for your love and support, and for running out to get me large bags of peanut butter M&M'S on those deadline weeks; to Hank and Ollie—steadfast writing companions; and to my family.

Finally, I'm hugely thankful for the readers, teachers, librarians, and booksellers who have shown me and my books such kindness.